Poppy Mayberry, Return to Power Academy

Nova Kids Book 2

Jennie K. Brown

Copyright © 2017 by Jennie K. Brown

POPPY MAYBERRY, RETURN TO POWER ACADEMY by Jennie K. Brown
All rights reserved. Published in the United States of America by Month9Books, LLC.
No part of this book may be used or reproduced in any manner whatsoever without written permission of the publisher, except in the case of brief quotations embodied in critical articles and reviews.

Hardcover ISBN: 978-1-946700-57-5
Trade Paperback ISBN: 978-1-945107-89-4
EPub ISBN: 978-1-946700-20-9
Mobipocket ISBN: 978-1-946700-21-6

Published by Tantrum Books for Month9Books, Raleigh, NC 27609
Cover Designed by Beetiful Book Covers
Cover Copyright © 2017 Tantrum Books for Month9Books

For Eddie
Love you honey bunches of oats

Poppy Mayberry,

Return to Power Academy

Nova Kids Book 2

Chapter One

The first time I got in trouble for using my fantabulous mind-reading Thursday power was when I was sitting in the middle of Mr. Salmon's sixth grade math class.

I almost missed the perfect mind reading opportunity because Mr. Salmon's giant toupee was bouncing on the top of his head as he walked across the front of the room, and this totally distracted me. I chuckled, thinking of its resemblance to a furry, gray squirrel just hanging out on his head.

"Psst," I heard from behind me. I turned around and saw Mark Masters. His index finger was jammed up his nose—it was a bad habit he hadn't been able to kick. I guess he has to be known for something since he is a powerless

Saturday. Mark's other hand pointed to the toupee king who now stood in front of me.

"Miss Mayberry," Mr. Salmon droned.

"Yes," I responded, polite as ever.

"Can you tell the class the square root of forty-nine?"

Of course, I knew the answer was seven. When in doubt, I always answer seven. I just love that number. Seven days in a week, after all.

"Seven," I said.

He grimaced and took a step closer to me. Did he really have to pick on me? He was a mind-reading Thursday and totally read the toupee thought out of my head—I was sure that was why he was attempting to call me out in the middle of class.

"Alright. That was an easy one," he said, pushing the thick wire-rimmed glasses up his nose. "Now tell everyone the square root of 657." A huge smirk formed on his face.

I thought back to our homework from last night, but nothing came to me. Sometimes I wished that my Monday power could conjure up answers just as quickly as it allowed me to move things with my mind.

I glanced over at my former archenemy, Ellie Preston, and tried to read the answer from her head. She shook her head two times, meaning she had no idea what the answer was. Ellie had many strengths, but mathematics was definitely not one of them.

"That's what I thought, Miss Mayberry," Mr. Salmon said through a smile. The class giggled.

As he turned his back to me and walked down the aisle, I read his mind, *that's what you get for making fun of my stylish hair.*

"I wouldn't call it stylish," I said quietly, not knowing what compelled me to say it aloud when I could have just thought it right back at him. I hoped he hadn't heard me, but the look in Mr. Salmon's eyes told me otherwise.

"Excuse me, Poppy?" Mr. Salmon said, walking back toward my seat. His hair bounced with each step and I chuckled to myself. At this point, all eyes were on me.

I responded confidently, "I just said I wouldn't call your hair stylish." Giggles came from every direction. Did I seriously just make fun of my teacher in front of the class? This would so not be good.

"I need to speak with you in the hall, Miss Mayberry," Mr. Salmon said, his tone deadly serious. He slicked down the furry madness on his head while a slight pink color dabbled his cheeks. The other Nova Middle students made all the typical *oohs* and *aahs* they make when anyone is sent out of the classroom.

"I know exactly what you did in there," he said, nodding his head toward the classroom door, "and I know you're getting used to this newfound Thursday-ness, but you know the rules about power usage in school!"

I could tell that Mr. Salmon was getting flustered, just like he did any time he had to yell at a student. He was so odd.

"It is one thing to read the thoughts from peoples' minds, but quite another to make those thoughts known!" he whisper-yelled, and his face began to turn an orangish-pink shade. "You don't want to spend another summer at Power Academy, do you?" he asked.

Of course I didn't want to go back there, but I couldn't stop staring at the color spreading across his face. "Mr. Salmon, you're turning salmon."

Mr. Salmon's hands shot up to his face. "I, umm, I … just don't do it again," he stammered, whipping around quickly and slamming the classroom door behind him. I just stood there, not knowing what to do next. I smiled to myself, thanking my lucky stars I didn't get sent to Principal Wobble-Wible's office.

That's when I, Poppy Rose Mayberry, realized that being a telekinetic Monday AND a telepathic Thursday could actually get me into trouble. But it could also be a lot of fun!

Chapter Two

Six Months Later

Now here I stood at Power Academy yet again. I laughed to myself as I stepped under the giant arch at the entrance of the Academy. Just like he did at last year's welcoming ceremony, greasy Mr. Grimeley was handing out squishy stress ball thingies that read *Embrace Your Day, Be Special.* Totally weird. Couldn't they be a bit more creative this year?

Grimeley himself didn't change much. His pants were still in good need of hemming—the bottoms curled under his unpolished shoes and made a swishing sound with every step he took.

It had been exactly one year since I entered the Academy for the first time. One year since meeting crazy Clothes-too-tight Headmistress Larriby and her greasy sidekick Mr. Grimeley. One year since I made new friends in Logan, a disappearing Friday, and Sam, a light-manipulating Wednesday. One year since my arch-nemesis, the mind-reading Thursday Ellie Preston, became one of my all-time favorite people. And, exactly one year since I found out that I am not only a telekinetic Monday, but also a mind-reading Thursday—a "cusper."

But after all the drama of last summer—crazy Larriby and greasy Grimeley hid Pickle, my adorable and furry little Yorkie—I definitely needed a little bit of convincing to come back this summer as a newly appointed camp counselor. And Ellie was the one to do just that.

"Poppy—if you aren't going with me, I will, like, seriously die," Ellie exaggerated, yet again, while plopping down on the giant purple Papasan chair in the corner of my bedroom. Pickle jumped up on her lap and begged to have her ears rubbed.

I looked at Ellie and frowned, thinking of what an embarrassment I had been at first with my lack of skills in the whole power department.

"Just think, Poppy. It's only six weeks this summer!" Ellie smiled at me, her legs now curled under her on the oversized chair. She was right. I could do six weeks. On the bright side, it was much better than being there for an entire summer.

"And then we can be back to lounging by the pool, sipping on lemonade?" I asked, and she nodded her assurance.

So after a bit of deliberation, I decided, what the heck? A few weeks at Power Academy couldn't be that bad, right? At least this time, we were getting paid.

Chapter Three

And so it began. Clothes-too-tight Headmistress Larriby wobbled her way down the center aisle of Power Academy's library. Today she looked like a rotting tomato. A giant rotting tomato, to be exact. The red dress hugged her curves in all the wrong places and was dotted with brown fluffy fabric. This was definitely not one of her best looks, although, from what I've seen of her, she's never had a good look at all.

I glanced around to see about thirty wannabe weekday students buzzing with anticipation. The Mondays were in a corner focusing, pointing fingers, squinting eyes, and attempting to make things move with their minds. To think I was one of them last year.

A group of Wednesdays stared at the light fixture in the middle of the room. I read their minds, but they were totally empty, putting every ounce of energy into their lack of power. All those poor Wednesdays wanted to do was flip the lights on and off a few times, but by the constipated looks on their faces, they were definitely struggling. Not even the slightest sparks flew from their fingertips.

"Psst." I turned around to see Logan suddenly appear behind me. My cheeks grew warm—they did that every time he showed up. He was just too cute. He nodded in Larriby's direction. I didn't have to be a mind-reading Thursday to know that he was thinking the same thing about her outfit as I was.

"Where have you been?" I whispered. I glanced at the clock to note it was 9:15, an hour later than when we were supposed to report.

"You know, got caught up at home with Gram and Pops," he said, smiling that crooked smile at me. Not only was he a disappearing Friday, but Logan also had the luxury of being one of the few teleporting Tuesdays at Power Academy. I'm happy that Logan had two powers to focus on. I mean, I kind of feel sorry for him; I can't imagine what I'd do if my parents were gone.

A piece of dirty blond bang fell into Logan's eye. With a simple flick of my wrist, I willed the hair to shoot straight back on his head. I chuckled at the Mr. Greasy Grimeley-esque comb over I just gave him.

"Thanks a lot, Poppy," he said through a smirk. His hand ruffled the hairs back into their original position. I remembered last summer when I could barely even move a feather with my mind. Now I'd practically perfected my power. Gone are the days of flying spaghetti sticking to my dad's bald head, out-of-control dog brushes hitting Pickle, and headbands violently shattering against chalkboards. Now when I use my powers and there's a disaster, it's on purpose.

"So has anyone talked to you about what we're actually doing here?" Logan asked.

"Nope, not at all," I said, pulling my out-of-control curly red hair into a messy bun, something Ellie had recently helped me perfect. Seriously, my hair was a disaster zone last year. "Mayor Masters said that we'd be helping the powerless and stuff, but she never mentioned the specifics," I said, looking over his shoulder. Clothes-too-tight Larriby and Mayor Masters (nose-picking Mark's mom and the Mayor of Nova) were having a heated discussion.

"Well, if it's anything like last year, I'm out," he said,

leaning back in his chair, arms crossed over his chest.

His comment brought me back to those few awful weeks at the prison that was Power Academy. In order to help us come into our weekday powers last summer, Larriby and Grimeley had hidden our personal items from us. My precious dog Pickle had been locked up in a cage in the middle of a supposedly haunted forest. In the end, I guess we did master our powers, and learned that we were cuspers.

"Who's that?" Logan asked, taking me from my thoughts. Waltzing down the middle of the library aisle was a man that had the letters N.P.C. stitched into the upper right pocket of his jacket. A wide-brimmed black hat was pulled low over his eyes. He was not your typical-looking Power Academy instructor, especially with those tight black skinny jeans (yuck), but for some reason, he looked familiar to me. As he lifted his head to talk to Headmistress Larriby, I realized exactly where I'd seen him before—when I'd told my other best friend, Veronica White, about my summer plans last week at Novalicious.

"So, you're telling me that you're going to spend every single day of the next two months at Power Academy?" Veronica blinked hard. "With Ellie?"

Veronica and I had been best friends since ... well ... forever, and she was still getting used to the fact that my ex-enemy Ellie Preston and I were now seeing eye to eye. I wanted to be completely honest with Veronica about the whole cusp power thing—something else I had in common with Ellie but not with her—but we had all promised Mayor Masters that we would keep that to ourselves. Even though Veronica had no clue about the whole mind-reading thing, she had definitely sensed a stronger connection between Ellie and me over the last year. I guess I couldn't blame her for being a little jealous.

"It's actually only six weeks," I said as I threw the Power Academy brochure down on the table in front of her. The bright greens and blues on the pamphlet made the place look pretty appealing—I was happy they'd revamped it from last year's.

Using her Monday power, Veronica pushed the pamphlet back to my side of the table and took a lick of her cone, totally avoiding eye contact. Did she have to be so dramatic?

I glanced around Novalicious and saw all sorts of other

people using their weekday powers. Neil Porter, a boy from my fifth period history class, used his telekinesis power to suspend three cones in mid-air as he reached for a fourth. After paying at the counter, Mr. Ellison and his son Trevor (both Tuesdays who frequented Novalicious) vanished into thin air. Obviously, they teleported back home.

I glanced back at Veronica just in time to see her smiling at me. She was back to her normal non-jealous self. "Look, Poppy. You are totally going to be fantabulous helping those other students," she stated in between bites of peanut butter, chocolate chip goodness. "I'm sorry I get a bit …" She stopped mid-sentence. Her eyes widened at the sight of whoever just walked through the glass door. "Look! Look! It's one of *them*," she said, wiping her face with the back of her hand. She nodded toward the entrance of Novalicious.

I turned around to see a tall, skinny man in a long black jacket shuffling through the line. On the upper right corner of his coat was a shield emblem containing the initials N.P.C. His black baseball cap had the same exact lettering.

"Those Nova Power Corp. guys totally freak me out," I whispered, leaning forward in my chair and away from him as he passed behind me.

"What about your dad?" Veronica asked. "Does he freak you out too?"

"Very funny." I said, unenthusiastically. My dad does work at Nova Power Corporation, but he's a security guard, not whatever this guy was. I stole a glance over my shoulder. The man's dark eyes scanned across Novalicious from one person to the next. I'd seen that look enough times to know that he was a mind-reading Thursday. When his eyes met mine, they lingered for just long enough to make a shiver run down my spine. My default thought, dog poop, entered my head.

"He's obviously looking for something," Veronica said, leaning closer to me.

I swallowed. "Or someone. *Dun. Dun. Dun.*"

The man got in line behind Mr. and Mrs. Ream, two poor, powerless weekends.

"Or maybe he's come to personally escort you to Power Academy," Veronica said with a giggle, lightening the mood even more.

"Yeah, right!" Over the last year, under the direction of Mayor Masters, Nova Power Corporation moved to the grounds of Power Academy due to some space issues. So while it wasn't entirely out of the question that he would venture outside of N.P.C. to pick up a measly Monday (and semi-Thursday), it was still laughable.

"What a weirdo!" Veronica said as we watched his head

move mechanically from side to side, scoping out the scene. Suddenly, the little ol' creepster whipped his head around toward us. This time his eyes lingered on me even longer than they did earlier.

"Oh. Em. Gee … do you think he heard us?" Veronica said.

"Nah. Just a coincidence," I said, but I wasn't entirely sure. Ever since he entered Novalicious, I had the strange feeling that he wasn't focusing on anyone but me.

Veronica pulled the hair tie from her ponytail and let a few black strands fall in front of her face. "Okay, for serious though. Now he is totally starting to creep me out," she whispered.

"Is he still looking in this direction?" I asked. The man had moved up in line, so now my back was to him.

Veronica's eyes slowly moved from my forehead and then up a bit farther. "Yep," she said without moving her lips. I really wanted to tell her about my new power.

"Let's finish up here," I said. Veronica and I licked our ice cream as fast as we could; my head started pounding from brain freeze.

I stood up and could now see the man sitting at a table near the only door in Novalicious with a glass of water. The odd man didn't even order a drink, let alone a cone, so there was no reason for him to be skulking around.

"Are you almost done?" I asked Veronica, grabbing the orange pendant suspended from my neck. My purple ballet flat tapped on the floor below. I wanted to get the out of here, and fast. With a quick twist at her hand, Veronica's trash lifted from her palm, gently flew across the room, and landed in the trash can directly to the strange guy's right.

We rushed out of Novalicious as quickly as our legs could carry us, but with each step, I could feel the man's eyes on me.

And then, it got even stranger. As we left, Mayor Masters flew past us without a hello or even a glance, which was odd considering we've been in school with her son for the past five years and she'd personally invited me to be a Power Academy counselor.

"Rude, much? Veronica said with an eye roll. "And how long have we been friends with Mark?"

I thought of the many times Veronica had not-so-subtly called Mark out on his, ahem, nose-picking habit.

"I didn't realize you considered him a friend," I said, not meaning for it to come out as harsh as it did.

"And what's that supposed to mean?" she said snarkily, stopping dead in her tracks.

"Nothing. Just forget about it," I said, hoping she would.

Ever since Ellie started hanging out with us, Veronica's been even more touchy than usual.

"I have to go," she spat, turning to walk in the opposite direction. "Say hi to your BFF Ellie for me." Her black combat-style boots stomped away.

Before I even had the chance to yell after her, Veronica had turned the corner and made her way out of sight. That was not the way I wanted to leave my best friend before six weeks away at Power Academy.

Now, that same creeper guy from Novalicious was here at Power Academy. I glanced at Clothes-too-tight Larriby just in time to see a scowl form on her face. Whoever this man was, she was not happy to see him. The mysterious man walked straight up to the stage and leaned in close to Larriby. Her face contorted into an even bigger frown as he whispered in her ear.

"Come on," Logan said, glancing in my direction. "Use your Thursday skills, Poppy. Larriby looks mad."

I concentrated really hard on Headmistress Larriby. I

wanted to see what she was thinking of this guy's comments. Typically when I did this, a few words flew through my head here and there and it was easy to get the gist of somebody's thoughts. But right now, I got nothing but static.

"Well?"

"Nothing," I said with a frown. "Too many other weekday thoughts flying around. It's distracting."

The strange man drew back from Larriby and then proceeded to walk back up the aisle in our direction. As he reached the row where I sat, his eyes caught mine just like they did at Novalicious.

"I wish he'd just go away," I whispered to Logan.

By the grimace on Headmistress Larriby's face, she didn't want him here, either.

Chapter Four

I brushed off the whole N.P.C. creeper dude incidents and headed to my dorm room to unpack some of my stuff. Ellie was already settled in.

"Did you really have to take the good bed again?" I asked with a smirk. Last summer she had commandeered the better of everything. Some things never change.

Ellie's bed was a perfect combo of soft and hard. My bed was lopsided and lumpy. Ellie's desk faced the window overlooking a cute little garden. My desk faced the dirty red brick wall. Ellie's dresser had seven perfectly working drawers. Two of the drawers in my bureau didn't even close the whole way—my underwear was exposed to anyone who walked into our room. I started opening and shutting her dresser drawers with my mind, laughing along with each push.

"Do you mind?" Ellie asked with a smile. She nodded quickly to the left and the drawers slammed shut. I kind of liked it when she only had the mind-reading power. The added telekinesis thing could get on my nerves.

"Has anyone talked to you about what we are going to be doing?" I asked.

Ellie plopped herself down on the fluorescent pink comforter. She grabbed a magazine from her pink bag and started flipping through the pages. This was much more important than some article about which shoes to wear with which shade of lipstick (yes, I totally used my Thursday power to see what article Ellie was reading).

I rolled my eyes. "Well, maybe Logan knows more than you."

"Oooh. Looogan," she said, puckering her lips. The mention of Logan seemed to get her attention.

Now it was my turn to ignore her, and I went back to stuffing clothes in my non-functioning drawers.

"Nobody has said anything. So why did we even agree to do this?"

She smirked. We both knew the reason.

"Oh, yeah. The money!"

It was totally for the money. Unless your parents are nice enough to give an allowance, which mine aren't, you can't even buy a cone at Novalicious without it. When Mayor Masters told us that we'd be paid 200 bucks for six weeks of working with powerless weekdays, I couldn't turn it down.

"It will be a good lesson in fiscal responsibility," my father had said over dinner after I'd agreed to the job, giving my mom an *aww-she's-getting-so-big* kind of smile. But I didn't know how responsible I wanted to be with it.

"What are you gonna do with the money?" Ellie asked, breaking my train of thought and obviously reading my mind.

"Not really sure, yet. But I have a few ideas." I looked down at Pickle and thought about a tiny dog carrier I had seen at Nova Pets-R-Us. It had purple and white stripes and a plush, fluffy lining on the base—it was absolutely perfect for my little Pickle.

"Well, I certainly hope you're not going to buy anything for that tiny critter you call a dog," she said, scooping Pickle up and gently petting her head. Pickle sighed and nuzzled closer to Ellie.

It was crazy to think that a year ago, Ellie would have

made that *tiny critter* remark just to upset me—and she would have meant it—but now, here she was, bonding with little Pickle. I smiled at her, thinking about how she used to literally kick Pickle away from her, and then I smiled even harder thinking about how far we'd come in our friendship.

Knock, knock, knock I heard on our door.

"It's Sam and Logan," Ellie said, pulling herself up into perfect Ellie Preston posture. She tossed the latest *Teen Weekday Magazine* back into her oversized pink bag.

"Hey guys!" I said, letting them in and shutting the door. It barely closed behind Sam's giant cowboy hat. Seriously, the boy never takes that thing off. I smiled after noticing he still wore that camouflage jacket—too funny. Ellie noticed it too. Before I knew it, her arms were wrapped around Sam.

"Ouch," Ellie squealed as the brim of Sam's cowboy hat banged her head. Ellie's cheeks turned pink; she was so crushing on Sam.

"Well, we got the four-one-one on the whole camp counselor situation," Logan said.

"Well, it's about time," I said, pulling Pickle onto my lap. She leaned her head down so I could scratch behind her left ear. Such a furry spoiled princess, and I was so glad I had permission to bring her back this year. Larriby totally owed me, after all.

"And?" Ellie said. She looked at Sam and patted the comforter next to her. He got the hint and sat down.

"Well, apparently, they need a bit of help in the power intensive classes this year," Sam said excitedly. "There are some really weak weekdays."

"Say that five times fast," Logan said.

Our eyes met and we laughed. Sam and Ellie rolled their eyes. Obviously, Logan and I had a superior sense of humor.

"Heard that," Ellie said, scooching closer to Sam.

The power intensive classes were held twice a day for an hour. It was a time devoted entirely to developing specific weekday powers. Last summer I was in Miss Maggie's Monday power intensive class. At the beginning of the summer, I could barely lift a pencil without taking out someone's eye, but by the end of our short stay, I could pull wooden planks from buildings, move one hundred pound bookcases, and effortlessly brush Pickle without even lifting a finger.

"Did they say anything about the dual power thing? Like when we are gonna find out more about them?" Ellie asked.

"Nothing about that in particular, but they did

mention that we should still keep the whole thing under wraps," Logan said. He pushed a few strands of hair from his face. I sighed. Maybe I had a bit of a crush on him, but he's the one who kissed my cheek on the last day of camp last summer.

Ellie sent me a knowing smirk.

I still couldn't understand why we still had to be so secretive about the cusp powers considering our parents, all of our teachers, and Mayor Masters knew. And yeah, we have two powers, and everyone else has one. What was the big deal?

"Larriby and Grimeley want to meet with us in ten minutes to discuss our roles here," Sam said. "In more detail," he added, mocking Grimeley's nasally voice.

"Picks, you stay here," I said, rubbing her belly. "And don't you get yourself lost this year."

We entered the library again, but this time, I took a moment to look around. Things definitely looked different. Last year, the entire place was crumbling in on itself. Torn wallpaper hung from the walls; the chandelier had about three bulbs burnt out; and there were gaps on shelves where books should have been.

Now, there wasn't a single open space in the cases. The overhead chandelier had been replaced with a more modern, working one with dangling glass pendants that sparkled in the light. The old green and maroon wallpaper had been stripped off and replaced with a coat of light blue paint, similar to the color that my and Ellie's dorm room had been painted.

I remembered my dad mentioning something about Nova Power Corporation donating some money to Power Academy because of the new, shared location. I was glad the library looked nicer since we would end up spending so much time meeting here.

"I'm sure you're all wondering exactly why you're here," we heard Mayor Masters say from the back of the room. She walked down the center aisle and took a position up front next to Clothes-too-tight Larriby. I could see where her daughter Miss Maggie Masters got her skinny frame. Mayor Masters stood next to the big-boned Larriby in a fitted navy suit with navy heels to match. She was the epitome of business chic. As mayor, I guess that's part of her job.

Ellie, Sam, and I found our seats at the front of the library. Since everyone in the room knew about cusp powers, Logan teleported to the seat next to me. Show-off.

"I'm sure Headmistress Larriby filled you in on the smaller details of your job here, but I just wanted to outline the expectations a bit more." Even though Mayor Masters said this with a smile, there was a serious undertone to her words.

"Your roles have changed a bit from what we previously envisioned," she continued. "In fact, you will be taking on a more creative role these next few weeks."

A more creative role? When we'd been asked to paint using our powers in last summer's Power intensive class, I'd accidentally made a blue-stained paintbrush smack my friend in the butt. That disaster and the self-portrait I made at Nova Middle were the most creative I'd been in the last year. In my portrait, I'd made my hair appear even puffier and brighter orange than it did in real life (if that's even possible) because I couldn't get the right ratio of red and yellow. Mrs. Sharple gave me a C-minus on that assignment, which I thought was totally harsh. Needless to say, art was definitely not my forte.

"Now don't get me wrong," Mayor Masters continued. "You will still serve as mentors to the developing weekdays, but there will be an additional challenge to your weeks."

Suddenly, the double doors behind us slammed. The four of us turned our heads to notice a man—the creepy Nova Power Corporation man to be exact—swiftly walking in our direction. Why was he even here?

Logan leaned over and whispered in my ear. "Shouldn't he be next door at N.P.C.?"

Mayor Masters nodded toward Headmistress Larriby, who took over. "I'd like to introduce you all to Mr. Harold Fluxnut," Larriby said, lacking any ounce of enthusiasm. She raised her hand toward the creepy N.P.C. dude to her left. "Unfortunately, Mr. Grimeley has taken a job outside of Power Academy so he will not be with us this year." Headmistress Larriby frowned as she spoke, and I noticed Mayor Masters smirk.

Darn! Ellie thought to me, sarcastically.

I didn't expect this. Larriby and Grimeley were practically attached at the hip. Greasy Grimeley must have found a good gig elsewhere.

Mr. Fluxnut curled his lips in a half-smile, revealing a series of yellow, crooked teeth. What was up with people and their odd facial features at Power Academy?

Mayor Masters stepped forward and spoke. "Although he spends most of his days working in the technology department at Nova Power Corporation next door, Mr. Fluxnut has a fond interest in the arts. Therefore, he has volunteered his time this summer to assist us in our theatrical efforts here at Power Academy." From the looks of him, I found it hard to believe.

Headmistress Larriby stepped forward, closer to us than Mayor Masters. "This past fall, Mayor Masters … I mean, I, asked Mr. Fluxnut to join our staff as the new director of the creative arts program."

Ellie and I looked at each other. What was she talking about? Since when was there a creative arts program at Power Academy?

"What creative arts program?" Sam asked, taking the words out of my mouth. Out of the four of us, Sam was definitely the least creative. He'd much rather spend his time hunting, fishing, or camping than anything remotely related to the creative arts.

Ellie and I shrugged in unison.

"We decided that there isn't enough creative freedom of expression here at Power Academy. And the last thing we want our students to think is that they are trapped in a power prison."

Without looking at Ellie, I heard her think, *that's what we thought of this place at the beginning of last summer*.

No kidding.

"Okay, now that the introductions are over, what is it you want *us* to do?" Sam spoke forcefully. I've always appreciated his straightforwardness.

"This summer, in addition to assisting your assigned weekday mentee, your time will be spent working with Mr. Fluxnut on Power Academy's debut production."

I rolled my eyes. She had to be kidding. Production only meant one thing—a play.

"Wait? A play?" Ellie squealed. "I've always wanted to star in a Broadway show."

I chuckled. Power Academy was far from Broadway. Ellie turned toward me, and a giant smile took over her entire face. I remembered back to the fall production at Nova Middle. Mrs. Flannagan directed *The Pirates of Penzance* and totally cut Ellie from the first round of auditions. Ellie brushed it off saying, "I never really wanted to act in some stupid middle school play anyway," but I knew, deep down, that she was really disappointed—I read the disappointment right out of her head.

Unlike Ellie though, I was not so thrilled; I thought we'd be helping the powerless weekdays master their powers. Logan frowned. I didn't have to read the boys' minds to know that they felt the same way I did.

"So, what's the play?" I asked, feigning interest. I didn't want to spoil Ellie's excitement.

"Would you like to tell them, Mr. Fluxnut?" Larriby said, stepping aside.

The man spoke. I don't know what exactly I expected him to sound like, but it was nothing like the voice that came out of his mouth. "I would love to tell them, Mrs. Larriby," he said in the most dramatic, flamboyant, high-pitched tone I'd ever heard come from the mouth of a grown man.

Mr. Fluxnut absolutely beamed now—a complete 180 from the creepy behavior I'd remembered from Novalicious. "This year, you will be performing Shakespeare's *A Midsummer Night's Dream*," he said, throwing his hands in the air. "I wanted to choose something magical with whimsy because of our purpose here at Power Academy," he continued. "And when Mayor Masters, *er*, Headmistress Larriby, asked me to use my talents for the benefit of the wannabe weekdays, I simply had to say yes. Yes. YES!"

Was this guy for real? First, I was certain this was the mc-creepster that Veronica and I had seen at Novalicious just a few days ago skulking in the corner. This was also the same man who obviously frightened Clothes-too-tight Larriby earlier today. And now, here he was drama-ing it up. When I spotted him at Novalicious, I figured he was a mind-reading Thursday, but now I wasn't so sure. After all, for the last three minutes I'd been sending him thoughts of Pickle's poo, and he hadn't turned up his nose once.

Ellie elbow-jabbed my side. "Stop, please," she said, turning up hers.

At least someone was reading my thoughts.

"Okay, so obviously, I will play the lead," Ellie said, flicking a few strands of dark brown hair behind her shoulders. Her posture straightened.

"Naturally, this is something for the students of Power Academy," Mr. Fluxnut said. "They are the ones here to master their powers." His voice lowered. "Not. You." And just as quickly as his voice dropped, it went right back up. "You will get a role of some kind, but your main purpose is to help the … *powerless* develop their skills."

I thought we'd simply be working with the students during the power intensive classes, but now we were expected to *direct* them through their weekday power through a play. Ugh.

Headmistress Larriby stepped in front of the N.P.C. guy. "Of course, you remember last year's challenge." She avoided our eyes as she spoke. And it was no wonder. Even though it'd been a year, all four of us still hadn't totally forgiven Clothes-too-tight Larriby and Greasy Grimeley for the challenge last year. Who steals a precious dog? I smiled, knowing that at least Pickle was probably curled up in her fluffy purple bed, safely dreaming away.

"Each of you will be working with one hopeful yet powerless weekday. You will rehearse with them and practice their power with them, and it is your duty to make sure they are fully prepared to show off their newfound ability when the show debuts at the end of the six-week program.

"But you must remember one thing," Mr. Fluxnut continued, his voice suddenly becoming serious. "Nobody can know about your dual powers. It's *imperative* that you continue to keep this to yourself."

"Why is it so *imperative*?" asked Sam, mocking Mr. Fluxnut's emphasis. Mr. Fluxnut squinted his little, beady eyes.

Headmistress Larriby jumped in. "Because it's come to our attention that someone in the Nova community— probably a Saturday or Sunday—has been …" I turned around to see Mayor Masters's head shaking vigorously from side to side. I looked back to the front of the room where Larriby slumped her shoulders, looking uncomfortable. "Well, never mind. Just keep it to yourself, just as you've been doing this past year."

Sam began to speak again, "But you haven't answer—"

"Enough," Larriby said, the loudness and power of her voice practically shaking the room. A book from a nearby shelf tumbled toward the ground. Using my Monday power, I caught it and willed it to go back in its proper spot. To think, a year ago, I would never have been able to do that.

"There will be no more discussion about your cusp powers. Mayor Masters has assured me there are no cusp students here this summer, so there is no reason it should even come up." Headmistress Larriby flopped herself down in the chair. I chuckled to myself, thinking about how I had accidently moved a chair from under her butt last summer, making her crash to the ground.

"Now let's continue discussing this play," Ellie said, obviously unaware of the awkwardness that just engulfed the room. I had to laugh at her naïveté.

"Yes. Yes. Let's do move on," Mr. Fluxnut continued. "Since you all did so well with last year's challenge, each of you will monitor the progress of your assigned weekday during the rehearsals and shows. As mentioned before, you will attend their power intensive class each day and work with them during rehearsal time. If your mentee is able to master his or her power by opening night, you will receive an added bonus."

"A bonus of what?" Sam said.

"A monetary bonus," Headmistress Larriby interjected. *I believe you want a new dog home for your mutt,* she thought to me. Then her eyes darted to the back of the room once more. "Now off you go," she said, pointing to the exit. "Your schedules will be in your rooms before you wake tomorrow morning."

I went to sleep that night unsure of what Power Academy had turned into and what it had in store for me these next few weeks.

Chapter Five

I woke up in the middle of the night to the sound of Ellie's light, breathy snores. If we were still enemies, I would have whipped out my purple cellphone and tape-recorded her snorts to be broadcast all over the Academy the next day, even though technology of any sort was forbidden at Power Academy.

I tapped on the comforter next to me, signaling Pickle to jump up. I rubbed her belly and then gave two scratches behind each of her ears. She pushed her head farther into my hand. Too cute. I glanced at the floor to see that, just as Larriby promised, our schedules had arrived.

Poppy Mayberry – Daily Schedule
Mentee – Sabrina Pennycoff

8:30-9:15: Breakfast in the Cafeteria

9:30–10:30: Rehearsal with Mr. Fluxnut

10:45-11:45: Monday power intensive class

12:00-1:00: Lunch

1:15-2:15: Monday power intensive class

2:30-4:00: Rehearsal with Mr. Fluxnut

4:15-5:30: Free time

5:45-7:00: Dinner

7:00–8:15: Additional rehearsal upon request of Mr. Fluxnut

8:30: Report to dorm room until morning

I sighed at all the rehearsal times, but at least we didn't have pointless classes. Last summer we had a History of Nova class every day, which was … well … useless. Meteor hit Nova. Yada, yada, yada. One meteor per day of the week. Yada, yada. Woke up to newfound powers. Yada. Same old, scripted stuff we learned every year since the first grade. And these lucky weekdays didn't have to power through it this year. Pun totally intended.

I glanced over to see a still-snoring Ellie and decided to use this extra time to explore Power Academy a bit while all remained quiet. Since I already saw the changes in the library, I wanted to check out what else was new.

Last year, we weren't allowed to leave our dorm rooms outside of specific time frames, probably because we didn't have much control over our powers back then; they didn't want electricity going on and off in the middle of the night or hopeful Mondays accidentally breaking windows. Still, I was really surprised that they didn't put many restrictions on us this year. Larriby and Grimeley, well, Fluxnut, must have thought a step above powerless weekdays warranted a bit more freedom. Or maybe they didn't want it to seem like such a prison.

I got to the bottom of the wooden staircase and found myself in the entryway once again. For some reason, it seemed a bit creepy without all of the other weekday students roaming around. The ceiling seemed extra high and the hallways extra dark. Pitch black, to be exact. If I were a Wednesday, I would simply light the hall with my finger, but that wasn't the case.

My eyes adjusted to the blackness. All of the main rooms and hallways branched from this grand foyer—the center of the Academy. The huge chandelier hanging in the center of the room boasted like one hundred crystals. There had been too much chaos upon arrival yesterday for me to even notice how beautiful it was. Next to the front entrance door was the pocket door to the library and the first hallway, where all of the classrooms were located. From the looks of my schedule, I'd be splitting my time between there and the newly constructed auditorium for rehearsals.

The next hallway contained not only the boys' dorm rooms but also the faculty apartments; I had absolutely no desire to explore that hallway. The last corridor seemed to be a wing of administration offices, where something caught my eye—a giant, sliding glass door. It looked out of place and really modern compared to the wooden doors in other parts of Power Academy. Naturally, I had to explore this a bit more, even though this was the only hallway forbidden to students and counselors.

I started my way down the administration wing. Labeled *Mrs. Mayella Larriby*, the first door on my left was that awful headmistress's office. The next door down was *Mr. Harold Fluxnut's* office. A shiver went down my spine—there was something outright creepy about that dude. The guy from Novalicious seemed so—different— from the flamboyant play director here at the Academy.

Shrugging, I tiptoed my way to the end of the hallway.

I took a final step forward at the sliding door, thinking it would open on its own when I got close. No such luck. *Ouch!* I banged my head smack in the middle of it. "Way to go, Poppy," I said to myself, rubbing the spot on my forehead that would surely turn into a huge goose egg by the afternoon.

I tapped my foot forward this time, hoping again that the glass door would budge. Nope. Finally, I attempted to use my Monday power to do the same thing. I concentrated hard. *Move. Move. Move.* Nope. That was strange. Now that I was almost twelve, my power worked whenever I willed it to. There was no reason it shouldn't work now.

Then I noticed why it wouldn't open to any of my commands, normal or Monday—directly to the right of it stood a tiny black box with a red blinking light. It seemed like I needed an access card to get the doors to slide open. Obviously, the only ones with a card like that would be N.P.C. workers. Go figure. Maybe Sam could use his Wednesday power to open it—if that would even work.

I was about to turn around and make my way back up to my room when I saw movement out of the corner of my eye. Even with his back toward me, I recognized the boy standing on the other side of the door—Mark Masters— Mayor Masters' nose-picking extraordinaire of a son. I took a step to the side so he couldn't see me. I could tell that he was having a conversation with someone else, but not a normal one. His face was bright red, and he was using huge arm movements. It almost looked like he was arguing with someone. And what was he doing here so early in the morning?

Suddenly, the other someone came into view. A short, stocky man in a Nova Power Corporation jacket had a vice-like grip on Mark's collar. I watched as Mark's right fist made contact with the man's forearm, but to no avail. The guy's arm didn't budge at all.

Even though I couldn't hear any talking through the thick door, I could still channel my Thursday power. "I don't want to go back there," Mark said, his head tilted toward another door. He tried to wriggle his way from the man's grasp but the short man continued to hold on.

He yanked Mark toward him so fast that his head snapped back in my direction. Mark's eyes locked with mine. Fear. Mark was afraid. I didn't hear him say it, but he was thinking *Help, Poppy.* Then the man wrenched forward and the two were out of sight, making their way somewhere into the Nova Power Corporation part of this ginormous building.

What the heck was that all about? I needed to find out, and I knew exactly who could help me.

Chapter Six

I filled Ellie, Logan, and Sam in on the incident with Mark over breakfast.

"And you're absolutely sure it was him?" Ellie said, using her cusp Monday power to slide the syrup down the table and right into my hand.

"Ellie!" I whisper-yelled.

"Relax, Poppy," she said, looking around the cafeteria. "Nobody noticed."

Thank goodness for that. She slid it back toward the middle of the table, further away from Sam.

"Um. Excuse me? I was about to use that," Sam said, reaching in the place where the syrup stood just seconds ago, before Ellie slid it away. Once he realized it was Ellie and not me who slid it from his grip, he smiled. He was totally crushing on her.

"I'm positive it was Mark," I said through chews of waffle goodness.

Sam lifted up his cowboy hat to scratch the side of his head. "You know, it was super late at night. Maybe you were sleepwalking or something?"

I rolled my eyes at him. That was just about the most ridiculous thing I'd ever heard. I've never sleepwalked in my life.

"No," I replied tersely. "I've been through every grade with him. I know it was him." I'd stared in awe at Mark digging for gold so many times that I could recognize him, his finger, and his nose anywhere.

"His Mom is the mayor of Nova, so don't you think she'd know if something fishy was going on?" Logan asked, suddenly appearing next to me. I hated when he just appeared like that, but I was glad to see him. My cheeks grew warm—until he looked up at me.

"Whoa! What happened to your head?" he asked, staring at the bump that I predicted would form after smashing my head on the glass.

"Anyway," I said, pouring more syrup on my breakfast

and ignoring his comment, "let's just keep a look out, okay? It was just plain weird."

They nodded in agreement and we got back to our waffles and strawberries.

After breakfast, we had our first "rehearsal" of the summer. I was excited to go because I could finally meet my mentee, Sabrina Pennycoff.

"Alright, alright! Let's hustle, please," Mr. Fluxnut announced, making his way down toward the stage in the new auditorium. He had changed out of his N.P.C. garb and was now dressed in skinny jeans and a t-shirt that read *World's Best Director*. Was that really necessary? I looked him up and down. Poor Mr. Fluxnut looked like he hadn't eaten in weeks. He was as thin as a candlestick, all skin and bones from his pointy chin the whole way down to his long, shoeless feet.

The weekday students were seated in the middle of the stage in a circle, arranged by day of the week. Mondays sat stage right, then the Wednesdays, Thursdays, and finally the

Fridays. Tuesdays didn't come into their teleporting power until they were thirteen (except for Logan, of course), so there were no Tuesdays at Power Academy.

"Now, where are my Wednesdays?" Mr. Fluxnut said, looking around the stage as if he wasn't the one to organize the seating.

"Because of your Wednesday electricity-manipulating powers, you will be in charge of the lighting, sound effects, and other technical elements of the play." He did a dramatic spin in the middle of the stage. "And you will be expected to do this *entirely* with your weekday powers, of course." He pursed his lips together and did a little humming laugh. The pressure was on for those poor Wednesdays.

Sam stood behind the struggling Wednesdays. He nodded at his mentee, Lester Manchester, a freckled-faced boy with black-rimmed glasses that looked just like Sam's.

Mondays were to master their telekinesis by opening night. In *A Midsummer Night's Dream,* they were playing the magical fairies and some of the actors in *Pyramus and Thisbe*—the play within the play. These were the most magical and whimsical roles, so it seemed appropriate for them to sprinkle fairy dust or propel objects across the stage using their Monday power instead of special effects. That could definitely become disastrous if these Mondays didn't get a hold of their powers by opening night. I was in charge of seeing that my mentee Sabrina Pennycoff did just that—and that she did that exceptionally well.

"Because Thursdays are supposed to read minds and don't actually have the power to do anything *tangible*," Mr. Fluxnut spoke with what sounded like disdain, "your job is to telepathically send lines to the other Thursdays. Therefore, you will be serving as stage managers and playing the roles of some of the main characters."

Phew. For some reason, I was under the impression that Ellie, Logan, Sam, and I would be playing some of those major roles. Thank goodness that wasn't the case.

"Except, of course, for our camp advisors," Mr. Fluxnut said, staring at me. If he weren't a Monday, I would have sworn he'd just read my mind.

"Logan Prince, you will play one of the leading male roles—Demetrius." He rolled his eyes in disgust yet again.

"The role of Helena will go to Ellie Preston."

"Oh-em-gee, my breakthrough performance! I will *not* disappoint you, Mr. Fluxnut," she squealed, pushing a few strands of chestnut hair that escaped from her headband out of her face.

Mr. Fluxnut raised and then lowered his arm—an attempt to get Ellie to calm down.

"Sam, I want you to portray Lysander."

I thought back to the synopsis of the play I read before rehearsal. That must mean that I would be playing the only other female lead, Hermia. Great.

"And Poppy Mayberry—you will be portraying the role of Robin Goodfellow—Puck."

What? "But isn't Puck a boy?" I asked, trying not to sound too disappointed.

"You will be a female Puck," he added, and before I knew it, his skinny, clammy fingers were in the spirally mess I like to call my hair. I grabbed my mom's orange pendant that I wore on a necklace—my security blanket, so to speak.

"I just think this hair would go to waste if you played a character like Hermia. Puck is much more fitting." He smiled, twirling a few orange strands around his fingers. "Much more magical," he said, dropping my hair from his hands. "Don't you think?"

Seriously, what did hair have to do with anything? Mr. Fluxnut was so weird. And why did a play have to be this year's challenge? The only other two plays I'd been in had been disast—

The buzzing of the overhead speaker broke my thought. *"The following individual is wanted in Headmistress*

Larriby's office," a voice bellowed from above.

They didn't even have to say the name. I knew who it was.

"Poppy Rose Mayberry"

I rolled my eyes, frustrated that I not only had to go to Larriby's office, but that I didn't get to meet Sabrina. What had I done, now?

Chapter Seven

The office door crashed behind me as Headmistress Larriby scuffled to her seat. Today, she wore the outfit that made her look like a giant eggplant. The too-tight, purple dress hugged her body in all the wrong places and she had a funny-looking, puffy green scarf tied around her neck. I knew that was too tight too, because a skin roll hung over it—a skin roll that seemed to have grown even larger over the past year. Yuck.

The last time I was in her office was at the end of Power Academy last year, when we found out about our cusp powers. Of course, I'd had a feeling about mine for some time before then; the conversation between Ellie, Logan,

Sam, Mayor Masters, and me just solidified it.

I glanced over at the bookshelf in the corner—and the secret compartment tucked behind it. Last summer, Miss Maggie had told me and some other Mondays an old secret to the school. Before Power Academy was converted into a school for the powerless, the building was used as a hospital. Hidden compartments where doctors kept medical supplies were tucked behind all sorts of furniture in classrooms and in offices.

"Look. I think we need to discuss something you saw early this morning," Clothes-too-tight Larriby said, wedging a fat finger between her scarf and her neck. When she lifted the green piece of fabric, a bright red line pressed into her skin. The scarf dug into her neck. It had to hurt.

"It doesn't," she said, obviously using her Thursday power to read my mind.

How embarrassing. "Sorry," I mumbled under my breath, ashamed that I had thought it. At least I didn't say it out loud. That had to count for something, right?

Headmistress Larriby sat down on the other side of her desk. "Don't you think we need to discuss that incident early this morning, Miss Mayberry?"

I blinked hard twice, trying to remember her last comment before I was so entranced by the scarf cutting off her circulation. Oh, yeah. Mark. "I … um … I don't know what you're talking about," I said. Of course, I knew exactly what she was referring to. My thoughts flashed back to Mark Masters standing on the other side of the glass door and how scared he looked when that crazy man grabbed him. How did Larriby even know about that? Oh, yeah. Hidden cameras. They were probably everywhere around here, and I was sure Larriby was watching every move we made.

Headmistress Larriby tugged at the green piece of fabric around her neck once more. It gave way a bit, and a hot breath of air burst from her mouth. She cleared her throat. "Miss Mayberry, even though you haven't exactly been the example Monday student, there are others much less fortunate than you.

"You see, those poor Saturdays and Sundays have no special talents. They go through life like any other normal, boring person who lives outside of our marvelous city." Her arm lifted a fat yet perfectly manicured finger toward the giant window to her right. "So here at Power Academy, and over at the N.P.C., we find certain jobs for those less fortunate." I'm sure the fact that Mark was the mayor's son played into his finding a job while other Saturdays and Sundays were homeless.

Larriby acted as if Saturdays and Sundays were the dregs of society, and a lot of people treated them that way. At Nova Middle, Mark Masters and Rylee Huckabee (a powerless Sunday) were always picked last for anything we did, whether in gym class or a group project, even though we were supposed to be equal in the public school setting. We weren't allowed to use our powers, but everyone did anyway, making the Saturdays and Sundays feel even more worthless. Poor Mark.

"But I saw that guy grab—"

"You THINK you saw a security guard grabbing Mark Masters, but in reality, he was just leading him back to work. You see, Mark has been selected for an internship program in maintenance, and he has been extremely resistant to this new appointment."

"Maintenance?" I asked. "You mean picking up trash and cleaning bathrooms? *Blech!*"

Clothes-too-tight Larriby squirmed in her seat. "Yes, that's exactly what I mean. Since he has some, um, connections, it was decided to give him some responsibility at Nova Power Corporation."

Although it was a reasonable explanation, I had a sense that Larriby was hiding something. And the way she said, *selected for the program.* Why wouldn't he elect for the internship, especially if it made him feel more special? What it was though, I had no clue. And as much as I wanted to question Headmistress Larriby right then and there, it probably wasn't in my best interest to do so. Not so early in the summer program, at least.

"Not only do I need to address the Mark incident with you, Miss Mayberry, but I also feel the need to remind you of what is prohibited here at the Academy." She looked me dead in the eyes. "Even though we are connected to the Nova Power Corporation, that does not mean you can feel free to explore the N.P.C. Headquarters at your leisure. Although attached, we are two entirely different entities. What occurs here is in complete separation from what occurs at N.P.C."

She leaned back in her chair and sighed. "There was no obligation for me to share that information with you, and it would be in your best interest to forget we had this conversation and move along with your advisory duties. You are here to do one thing, and one thing alone ... help those poor Mondays with their powers."

"But that guy with Mark—"

"That guy NOTHING," she said. The redness in her face became more pronounced as she held my gaze. "As far as you're concerned, that never occurred." And this was when her tone became downright cruel. "And if you so much as mention it again, you will be removed from campus, and I will ensure that you do not get paid for your time here." She paused and a smile spread across her face.

I swallowed hard. How could she ensure anything of the sort? She had no power over that stuff, so what made her think she could speak to me that way?

"Oh, I will be keeping an especially close eye on you, Miss Mayberry. You can be sure of that." She turned around in her chair, dismissing me.

I guess I was back on Clothes-too-tight Larriby's hate-list. Ugh.

As I opened the door to leave, I bumped into a smirking Mayor Masters who rushed into Larriby's office.

"Poppy," she said, nodding.

I slowed my pace. I sensed that Larriby felt uneasy about something, and I wanted a second to read her thoughts. I didn't think it was about me, but there was definitely something else going on here. The door slammed behind me before I was able to figure it out.

Chapter Eight

The whole walk up to my room, I couldn't stop thinking about Mark. The face he made. The plea for help. It definitely did not seem like he wanted to be there. And what was he doing there so early? Was it a custodial overnight shift? Headmistress Larriby just didn't have me convinced. But I had other things to think about.

I shrugged it off and opened my dorm door. "I just can't put my finger on it," I said to Pickle. Of course she had no clue what I was talking about, so I got a bark and a lick on the cheek. Pickle was so excited to see me. After tossing the *Embrace Your Day, Be Special* ball with her a few times, I headed to the power intensive class with my favorite Power Academy teacher ever, Miss Maggie. Last year, she helped me find Pickle and rooted for me during the whole ordeal. Not only was I excited to see her, but I was also super excited to meet my mentee, Sabrina.

"Pah-ppy," Miss Maggie and her British accent greeted me. Her skinny bird-like arms wrapped me in a hug.

"And how is that power coming along?" she asked with a wink. I knew she wasn't talking about my Monday one.

"Great!" I said. And that was the truth.

I knew you'd be fine, Miss Maggie thought.

I sat down next to my mentee, Sabrina Pennycoff. I could already tell that she definitely had some work to do in the Monday power department. It made me think back to my total ineptness last year. In fact, Sabrina reminded me of … well … me, in general. She was probably around the same height and weight as me, and her rosy cheeks were too cute. Her hair couldn't contrast mine more, though. It was light blond and just barely brushed her small shoulders.

"Hi, Poppy," she said sheepishly, sinking into her chair. Now I was certain she was petite like me, too—she was barely able to rest her elbows on the table. "I'm Sabrina," she said, and her cheeks became redder. The poor girl was nervous. I thought back to my first day at Power Academy and understood why she'd be anxious. There's a lot of pressure on wannabe weekdays.

"Welcome," I heard Miss Maggie's British accent say from the back of the room. Just like last year, a piece of chalk flew through the air above our heads, and, using her Monday power, Miss Maggie wrote her name on the front board.

I heard "oohs" and "aahs" coming from the six other Mondays. I remembered the feeling the first time she did that. *Oh, I wish I were like her*, I read from Sabrina's mind. I smiled. Didn't we all?

"You are all here for a very special reason," Miss Maggie began. "You want to show your full Monday potential, and I am going to help you do that." She smiled widely. Her energy almost made me believe her even though I knew that one or two of these students would never master their Monday power. Those two hopeless souls might as well have been born on a Saturday or Sunday. And here I sat with two powers. Sometimes I wished I could give some of my power to the powerless. I frowned, knowing that was impossible.

"I'd like to start this class with an exercise to gauge where you all are in regards to your Monday ability." She did the "come here" finger movement and nodded in my direction. "Poppy, please come up here and assist me."

All eyes were on me as I made my way to the front of the room. I didn't expect Miss Maggie to make me the center of attention this first day.

"Poppy was in your shoes last year at this time. She could barely lift a feather without using her hands," she said through a chuckle. "But after just over a week of intense classes and workshops, Poppy mastered her telekinesis with ease."

"Wow!" a voice exclaimed from the back of the room. "Only a week?"

I smiled, loving how Miss Maggie neglected to mention the whole stealing-my-dog-as-an-extra-incentive thing.

She smiled at me again. "Show them."

Miss Maggie's hand flew up and she pointed toward a bucket of red paint, a row of brushes, and white pieces of paper. They hovered in the air on her Monday direction.

She explained what I was to do with these through her thoughts.

As if Miss Maggie and I had planned this prior to class, using my telekinesis, I did just as she instructed in my head. In a flick of my wrist, I placed a piece of paper, brush, and cup of red paint in front of each of the Monday students. Because Sabrina was my mentee, I gave her a little extra paint. No one seemed to notice.

"And now, just as I did with the chalk, you will do the same with the brush and paint. Write your names on the blank sheet Poppy so aptly placed in front of you," she continued, beaming.

Last year, our opening challenge was to simply move a glass of water. The only mess we made was cleaned up in a matter of seconds. Giving these struggling Mondays an assignment like this invited disaster.

And I was right. Within a matter of two seconds, all heck broke loose. The boy seated in front of Sabrina, Hunter McKelly, stared intently at his brush, willing it to move. Instead, his cup of paint slid sharply to the left and tumbled onto his clean pants. A few of the other Mondays laughed. "Great," he muttered, as Miss Maggie sent a roll of paper towels across the room to him. But he looked down at just the right time, and the roll smacked him across the face. More laughing.

Caleb Wagner had just as much luck. He used his hands to dip the brush in the paint, and then he tried to telekinetically write with it. In a sudden movement, the brush flew across the room and smacked Morgan Dankers across the face.

"Hey!" Morgan shrieked, breaking her concentration.

Then there was Omar Jafrey. He did get his brush to move ... but not to the right place. It lifted from the desk and slapped Sabrina on the back of the head.

And just when I thought it couldn't get much worse, it did. In fact, it became an utter disaster area, as these poor Mondays struggled to get a handle on their unstable telekinesis power.

If someone were to look in the classroom window at that moment, they would have seen brushes, all with a coat of red paint, flying around the room smacking various Mondays. I looked down to see a red splotch on the side of my leg. *Great.*

Morgan was crouched under the desk, dodging gobs of flying paint. Shrieks and screams came from every direction.

The out-of-control brushes that weren't smacking other Mondays were smashing into walls, leaving red streaks behind. It looked like a bloodbath! Caleb ran around the room while screaming at the top of his lungs, dodging flying drawing utensils. But throughout it all, the Monday students were laughing hard. Even with ruined clothes and paint-laden hair, nobody was upset in the least.

Then there was Miss Maggie standing in the middle of the mess, frazzled. She sent rolls of paper towels to various parts of the room so the Mondays could begin cleaning up, but the Mondays were too busy trying to control their own tools to even begin cleaning.

"Enough!" yelled Miss Maggie. Everyone snapped to attention and the tools came crashing to the ground. Miss Maggie's face was bright red. She did not look happy. But then she surprised me. Just when I thought Miss Maggie was going to begin yelling at her class of powerless rejects, a short, high-pitched squeal escaped from her lips. And then another. And another. She was laughing. Laughing harder then I'd ever seen her laugh before.

Then Morgan started to laugh, and then Hunter, and then Sabrina, and then the rest of the students. I joined in.

When the giggles finally died down, Miss Maggie spoke. "And that was your true challenge," she said. "You need to let go of your fears and approach your power with open arms," she said. What great advice.

And she was right. These Mondays were so distracted with what was going on around them that they didn't have time to worry about how well they controlled their Monday power—they simply used it.

Miss Maggie smiled. "And look on the bright side of this mess. Even though it was disastrous, at least you were able to make things move."

I guess there was hope for them after all. Well, most of them. One of the poor Mondays sat in the corner the entire time though, just squinting away at her paintbrush.

After spending the rest of the time cleaning the mess, it was time to pack up.

"How long did it take you to get so good?" Sabrina asked, wiping the final streaks of red from her forehead.

"It took me until like the end of summer to really get good," I said. I used my Monday power and pulled the brush from her paint cup. In a few effortless swoops, I wrote her name on the top of her art paper.

She gasped. "See. That's exactly what I want to be able to do!" she exclaimed.

"It will come," I said. "I promise."

She smiled meekly at me and then her lips turned down. I didn't have to use my Thursday cusp power to know that she didn't believe me. Could I blame her?

As much as I wanted to be a Monday last year, I didn't have much confidence in my skills when I first started, either. Heck, just being sent to Power Academy was a huge blow to my ego—everyone talks about the powerless rejects who are forced to go. Nobody ever focuses on how good they are when they come out.

Before I turned to leave, I read something else in Sabrina's mind that was totally unexpected. *Maybe I should tell Poppy about* ... And then her thought trailed off. I was sure whatever she thought about telling me would come out eventually.

Chapter Nine

I had performed in front of an audience two times in my life. First, when I was in second grade and was cast as an elf in my class production of *The Elves and the Shoemaker*. The day we were to perform in front of our friends and family, I came down with an awful stomach bug. My mom and dad forced me to go to the show, even though I was totally down for the count. Just as I was about to speak my first line, I threw up. On my shoes. On my apron. On Ellie, who was playing the Shoemaker's wife. Everywhere. I was beyond mortified.

The other time was during our production of *Peter Pan,* the only time students were actually allowed to use their weekday powers at school. I was playing one of the lost boys. The Mondays were supposed to use their powers to make books, pens, pencils, and other school supplies fly around during the "I don't want to go to school" line of the song "I Won't Grow Up." Well, I hadn't mastered my power yet, so when it was my turn, my props just sat there in the middle of the stage. *Aw* sounds and mutterings of "that poor girl" escaped from the crowd—they obviously felt sorry for me and my powerless, castoff self. At the time, Ellie had gotten a kick out of that little disaster.

Therefore, it was a total surprise to me when Mr. Fluxnut announced that I would be playing Puck—the lead fairy of the fairy kingdom—in this summer's production. I hadn't had much luck with sprightly, magical creatures in the past, but obviously he didn't know that little tidbit.

"Now, let's pick up where we left off earlier, shall we?" Mr. Fluxnut said, pointing to a page in his script. Since it was only the second day of Power Academy, we were still reading through the script. Because of Shakespeare's crazy difficult language, it'd been taking us a while.

Today, Mr. Fluxnut wore even skinnier jeans than yesterday, which was nearly impossible. They clung to him tighter than all of the headmistress's tight outfits combined into one form-fitting getup. But, as always, he wore that

N.P.C. hat. I shivered. That hat reminded me of the whole Mark Masters thing I saw—whatever that was.

"Earth to Poppy," Ellie said, jarring me from my thoughts.

The students were chuckling, picking up on my spacing out.

"Sorry," I muttered, trying to find my place in the script.

Page 12, Logan said to me. I caught his eyes, which squinted from a smile. Gosh, he was cute.

Thanks, I mouthed.

"How now, Spirit? Whither wander you?" I said, lacking any ounce of enthusiasm.

"No, No, NO." Mr. Fluxnut said, getting louder with each *no.*

"Like this," Mr. Fluxnut said, hunching his body over and craning his neck forward in one of the most uncomfortable-looking positions I'd ever seen. "How now, Spirit? Whither wander you?" Now, I wasn't entirely sure what Puck was supposed to look like, but I was pretty sure he shouldn't be hunched over like a hobbit. I saw him as more of a magical, whimsical creature, not whatever this *thing* Mr. Fluxnut was doing in front of me.

"Yes, exactly like that," Mr. Fluxnut said to … well … himself.

Ugh. I was not getting the hang of this whole acting thing.

"Now try it again," Mr. Fluxnut said, swooping his arm in a figure eight motion and stepping back from me, allowing me to take my place center stage.

All eyes were on me. Seriously, this was more nerve-racking than last year's pressure to master my Monday power.

You got this, Poppy, I heard Ellie say in my head. Thank goodness for my cusp power.

I wrapped my fingers around the pendant suspended from my neck. After a deep breath I began, bending over slightly. "How now, spirit? Whither wander you?"

Mr. Fluxnut smiled, revealing his buttery teeth. "Much better! Let's move on!"

Silence.

"Now, where's my Fairy One?" His eyes darted around the stage.

The Fairy One he was looking for was Sabrina, my mentee. She pulled a bobby pin from her hair and used it to pick the dirt out of her shoes. She looked just as excited to be here as I was.

"Miss Pennycoff?" Mr. Fluxnut pointed a scraggly finger in her direction and in a gust of wind, her script turned to page fourteen.

Sabrina Pennycoff's wind-blown head snapped up to attention. She read from the middle of the page. "Either I mistake your shape—"

"Not there, Miss Pennycoff!" Mr. Fluxnut huffed. "Can someone please show her where she should begin?"

Silence.

Line two, I said in my head, even though she wasn't a Thursday and wouldn't hear me.

Her large brown eyes met mine for a split second and then she began. "Over hill, over dale. Thorough bush, thorough brier."

If took me a moment to realize that no one had told her where to begin. Did she just read my mind? I quickly threw that thought out of my head. No way. Larriby assured us we were the only cuspers at Power Academy this summer. That would be ridiculous!

Mr. Fluxnut grimaced. "No, no, NO," he said again, throwing his script to the floor. "Obviously you don't understand your characters at all."

His arm rose, and in another gust of wind the side stage doors flew open to reveal a spread of trees outside.

"You are playing vibrant, magical creatures." His eyes darted from person to person. "You have energy, vivaciousness, and exuberance."

I didn't know what those last two words meant, but I was pretty sure it was something exciting. And overly dramatic, of course. Drama seemed to be this guy's middle name.

"We need an exercise to get you all into character." He tapped his pointer finger on his chin. "Your characters live in nature. In the forest. So tomorrow, everyone grab your scripts. We're going outside for inspiration."

To the tune of "London Bridge is Falling Down", he sang, "To the forest we shall go." This man was crazy.

And although Mr. Fluxnut said this would be fun and fantastic, my memories of the haunted forest were anything but.

Chapter Ten

I knew that I wanted Sabrina to master her power well before the performance of *A Midsummer Night's Dream*, so I decided it would be best to meet during our lunch the next day. Not only that, but I wanted to get to know her a little better. It wasn't as if Headmistress Larriby left us much room in our schedule to do that.

"So what can we work on today?" Sabrina asked. We were on the front lawn of the Academy, right in front of the giant entry arches, sitting in the bright green grass.

"I was thinking we could just start with something light. Something simple," I said, unclasping the leash from around Pickle's neck. I rubbed behind Pickle's ears. "Now, don't you run away, girl!"

Sabrina grabbed the two ends of the open collar and pushed the plastic clasp together.

"Do you really think I'm going to let you do it that way?" I asked, using my Monday power to pull the collar from Sabrina's hands. With my telekinesis, I opened the collar once again and then set it down in the grass between us.

"Using your Monday power, I want you to gently lift the collar from the ground and clasp it around Pickle's neck."

Sabrina's nose scrunched. "But what if I pull it too tight?" she asked.

"You won't. I'm here to help you out if I need to," I said, giving her a reassuring smile.

The purple collar still rested between us. Pickle's tail wagged. She probably thought she was getting a treat. Poor girl. "Soon," I said, rubbing her ears again, sure she could smell the tiny bone-shaped treat burning a hole in the pocket of my skinny jeans.

I looked up at Sabrina. I could tell she was concentrating really hard because she squinted her eyes so hard they were almost closed. *Move. Move. Move,* I could hear her think.

"Sometimes it helps if you point to the object you want to—" Before I could even finish the sentence, Sabrina's finger pointed at the collar.

Move. Move. Move, she continued to say in her head. The collar didn't even budge an inch.

"I'm sorry, Poppy. I'm just not concentrating enough today." She picked up the collar with her hands and handed it to me. "Here," she said, shoving it my way. "You put it on," she said with a frown.

"Look Sabrina. I know you think that these powers will never come in, but you have to trust me." I leaned in closer to her. "Even though it was a hilarious disaster in Miss Maggie's class yesterday, you *could* at least move things with your mind. Not to the places you wanted. But you could do it." I thought about some of the other powerless kids in her class, like the one who sat in the corner and couldn't move anything at all. I knew Sabrina would be a fantabulous Monday one day.

Sabrina's eyes focused on the ground in front of her and then she looked at me and nodded, almost as if she knew what I just thought.

"So let's take a break from this for now," I said, picking up Pickle and putting her in my lap.

"I like that idea," said Sabrina.

"So what days are your parents?" I asked.

"My dad is a Tuesday," she said and paused. She picked

up a few blades of grass and twisted them in her fingers.

"And what about your mom?" I pushed.

"Well … um … she's a weekend," her voice trailed off. Obviously, Sabrina was ashamed of that. I had to admit that it's a bit weird to hear of couples that have one weekday and one weekend. Typically, married parents are either both weekdays or both weekends. I really wished that it didn't matter what day of the week you're born and that everyone saw each other as equal no matter if they could teleport, mind read, disappear, or have no magical powers at all.

"Well, I'm sure they are both great," I said. "I mean, they have to be pretty cool to have a daughter like you."

Sabrina smiled.

"So do you want to try again?" I asked, putting the open collar back on the ground.

"I guess so," she said, straightening her body.

"Now concentrate really hard," I said.

Her eyes squinted tight just like they did before, and I could hear her thinking, *Lift up now. Lift up now. Lift up now.*

I didn't know if it was my little pep talk or if she truly concentrated harder, but this time, the collar wobbled and then lifted about an inch from the ground.

It fell just as quickly as it lifted, though, when Ellie

yelled. "Hey, Poppy!" I frowned at Sabrina. If she only had a few more seconds, she could have totally gotten the collar around Pickle's furry neck.

"Hey, Ellie." I said, turning around to see Ellie dressed in pink (duh) from head to toe. Her Thursday mentee, Shelby Plattworth, trailed closely behind her and looked like a mini version of Ellie, with dark brown hair and a pink tunic with leggings.

"We're just on our way to Fluxnut's rehearsal in the haunted forest. Do you wanna walk to with us?" Ellie asked.

I read out of Sabrina's head that she didn't want us to walk alone, and I read from Ellie's that she could use the extra company. Last summer, I was a little afraid as we made our way through the forest looking for our stolen items (that we eventually recovered from a beat-up old shed), but the most terrified of us all was Ellie—I remembered how she dug her nails into my arm so hard that she left half-moon imprints in my skin.

It was rumored—and repeated over and over again by Veronica—that a Wednesday had gone missing after Larriby kicked him out of Power Academy two years ago and made him spend the night in the forest. Some thought he ran away, but most people were convinced that wild animals ate him.

Knowing that we were about to have a rehearsal in broad daylight though, I had a feeling that this trip to the haunted forest would be much less terrifying than last year's venture. I sure hoped so, at least.

Chapter Eleven

There's always a weird feeling I get when I go to any place that claims to be haunted—a shudder trickled through my body as I put Pickle in her den and had a seat.

"Now," Mr. Fluxnut said, waving his hands about. "In order to really grasp your characters, you need to *be one* with your characters." When he said the word *one*, it looked as if his eyeballs were going to pop out of their sockets.

Is this guy even for real? Ellie thought to me. I smirked and took a seat next to Logan on the lush grass. He scooted closer to me. So close, I thought our hands were going to touch. My cheeks burned.

"Miss Mayberry, can you please focus?" Mr. Fluxnut

asked, taking me from my thoughts of Logan. I had been staring at the two-inch green space between Logan and my almost-touching hands.

"Erhm, sorry," I muttered. "I'm ready, Mr. Fluxnut."

"Good. You are to be a model student, so please do act like one," he said snarkily, the fun drama gone from his tone.

Logan bridged the two-inch gap between our fingers and squeezed my hand gently. I could feel my cheeks burn even hotter and smiled shyly at him. I grabbed my orange necklace with my other hand and closed my eyes. I wanted to imprint this moment in my memory—the first time I'd ever held a boy's hand.

My enjoyment of the moment came to a screeching halt with the equally screeching sound of Mr. Fluxnut's voice. "This is a magical play! Fairies are everywhere. For this fantastical exercise, you will be birds lifting off in flight."

We all stared at Mr. Fluxnut, unsure of what he meant.

"Go now. Fly, birdies, fly!" Mr. Fluxnut started flapping his arms, lifting his knees high to his chest and squawking while twirling around in a circle. How the heck was this becoming *one* with our characters? It was more like making complete fools of ourselves.

Ellie thought the same thing as me.

"Go on. You try." I hoped he didn't want us to do this

for too long. I was in my favorite purple ballet flats, and although I'm not typically prissy about getting dirty, I did not want lime green grass stains dotting the tops of them. Plus, I didn't want to let go of Logan's hand.

Since I was the "role model" for the learning Mondays and had to serve a good example for Sabrina, I started my bird dance. I hunched my back, flapped my arms, and mimicked Mr. Fluxnut's high-pitched vocals. After about fifteen seconds, Ellie jumped in. She flapped her arms vigorously, whirls of pink encircling her. The rest of the students joined in on the awkwardness, and even I had to admit that this actually wasn't half bad. In fact, it distracted me from everything else that was going on. I didn't worry about the way I left things with Veronica outside of Novalicious, Larriby's threats, or the weird encounter with Mark Masters (which still seemed fishy to me). As I screeched around the rehearsal space and passed by the other weekdays, I noticed that someone was missing.

"Excuse me, Mr. Fluxnut?" I said, straightening out. I had broken the weird-squawking-bird character, and I had a feeling he wouldn't be happy about that.

"Why are you not being *one* with your magical personality, Puck?" he asked in a huff.

"I'm sorry," I said, scanning the nesting space again.

"I'm just wondering where Sam is."

"Sam who?" he asked, obviously miffed that I was interrupting his amazing rehearsal technique.

"You know. Sam Bricker. The Wednesday playing Lysander." Of course he knew who Sam was.

"Oh, yes, yes, yes. I'm not really sure," he said, brushing me off and then continuing his little birdlike prance. I could tell he was avoiding the question.

I looked at Ellie, who was completely engrossed in the bird exercise, her arms flapping away while Shelby pranced in circles around her.

And then I got Logan's attention. He cocked his head to the side and creased his eyes. *He wouldn't just not show up,* Logan thought to me.

"Something's up," I mouthed right back.

So where could he be?

I strutted over to Logan.

"He was here this morning," Logan said. "And I saw him after power intensive class and after lunch."

I glanced up to see Mr. Fluxnut staring in the direction of the Nova Power Corporation. I followed his gaze. Two men were rushing toward him, and one of them was the guy I saw arguing with Mark Masters. Mayor Masters followed closely behind.

There seems to be a situation, I heard the one man think.

"There seems to be a situation," he then said aloud to Mr. Fluxnut.

The two men surrounded Mr. Fluxnut. He swiftly turned on his toes and headed back to N.P.C. with them.

It was a frazzled Mayor Masters who dismissed us for the rest of the afternoon.

"It's just so weird," said Logan. We were in his and Sam's dorm room. I could see that whenever Sam left, he did so in a rush.

His bed was full of empty chip wrappers, greasy, finger-stained hunting magazine, and clothing. He didn't even take the time to clean up a bit. His dresser drawers overflowed with clothing of all sorts of colors. Two more magazines—one about hunting and one about woodwind instruments, still in their original wrappers—sat on the top. It was obvious he didn't pack a thing, and the evidence showed that he didn't expect to leave Power Academy anytime soon.

"What about his bathroom stuff? You know, the essentials?" I asked, pushing the trash to the floor so I had room to sit down.

Logan shook his head. "I looked earlier. Toothbrush, toothpaste, soap. It's all there." He frowned and shook his head. "Everything's still there."

"Yeah," Ellie said. "It's almost as if he disappeared."

"And that's my job," Logan said, cracking a smile.

Ellie rolled her eyes. "Ha, ha, ha," she said without an ounce of humor.

"Maybe he had an emergency at home," I offered, but deep down, I knew I was wrong. Something felt off. Just like it felt off last year with the whole Pickle situation. I should never have decided to come back to this place. Maybe I should just get out of here now. Pickle whined, as if she knew that I needed some snuggles right now.

"They aren't telling us something," Logan said.

"Yeah. Did you see the way those N.P.C. guys showed up today? That was just plain weird." Ellie said.

"Maybe we should ask Larriby or Masters what's going on?" Logan offered.

"I'm already in enough trouble with Larriby as it is. There's no way I'm gonna ask her about this," I said.

"Then let's just listen in as best we can today and see

what we get," Ellie said to me. This was a logical idea. I had a Thursday power, after all. I might as well use it to listen in on thoughts. Sometimes my ditzy friend surprised me.

"We will figure this out," Logan said, pulling me in for a hug. "But first, I told Deklan I would meet with him about an assignment we have from our Friday Power intensive class."

I so wanted to believe him when he said we would figure this out.

Ellie left to go rehearse her part with Shelby, so I decided to head back to our room to cuddle with Pickle and work out one of my problems. Between Monday Power intensive classes and twice-daily rehearsals with crazy Mr. Fluxnut, I hadn't had much to time to think about the situation with Veronica.

This was the first time we'd gone more than a day without talking at all since we met way back in second grade. Sure, we've had minor disagreements here and there over stupid stuff like having the same crush or getting to eat the last slice of pizza. But I don't ever remember her walking away from me like she did right before I left for Power Academy.

I thought back to how mean Ellie had been to me over the last few years before we became friends—tripping me in the cafeteria, nailing me in the head with tennis balls during gym class, trying to steal Logan and my other friends away from me. To think Ellie did all of that because she was jealous of my Monday powers—her mother wanted her to be a telekinetic Monday like her, not a mind-reading Thursday. And now Veronica was dealing with the same jealousy issues herself. I needed to fix this; Veronica and I had been best friends since the second grade, and I never wanted to lose a friend like her.

It had been bothering me how we left things before I left for Power Academy, and now I was ready to move on from that. Because we weren't allowed to bring cell phones to Power Academy, I couldn't just text her like I normally would. Last summer we sent letters back and forth, so I figured I would do that again. This would help distract me from the Sam situation, too. Pickle curled up next to me as I began to write.

> *Dear BFF Veronica,*
>
> *I know the way we left things was a little rough. I'm sorry if I made you upset in any way. I didn't mean to snap at you over the whole Mark Masters comment. I know that you don't really like Ellie, but you should give*

her a chance. She really isn't as bad as you think. Those things last year were just flukes.

It's only week two here, and there has been weird stuff happening already. I will tell you more in person, but Sam just left, completely out of nowhere, and it just seems so strange. And these creepy N.P.C. dudes are always skulking around—they're up to no good.

I stopped writing, wanting so badly to tell her about my cusp power and that I can read minds on top of moving things telekinetically. But then, I thought back to Larriby and Mayor Masters and Mr. Fluxnut and their insistence on keeping it under wraps for now. I still didn't understand why. I mean, Mayor Masters said that we'd learn more about our powers this year. But we hadn't learned much about them at all. I pushed it out of my head and kept writing.

On top of all the weird stuff, I have to act in this play (which, by the way, seems like a total waste of time for all of us), and you know how acting has gone for me in the past. Total. Train. Wreck. What's even worse is that the creeper guy we saw at Novalicious is the director. Didn't expect that at all. But I still feel like he was watching us that day.

Anyway, I know you're mad, but please write back. I miss you. I miss my best friend.
Love,
Poppy

I folded up the letter and instead of putting it in an envelope, I tucked it into my back pocket. I knew that Logan would probably be teleporting home at some point over the next day or two, so it seemed easier for him to deliver it that way.

Chapter Twelve

The next two days flew by. During that time, neither Logan, Ellie or I heard a thing about Sam, and whenever Ellie or I attempted to read Larriby's or Mr. Fluxnut's thoughts, it all came up blank. Total blank slate.

Mr. Fluxnut thought about weird drama exercises, like, all of the time, and Larriby's thoughts usually revolved around stuffing her face full of food. No surprise there.

What was even stranger than Sam's disappearance was the fact that three hours later, Logan said that two N.P.C. guys barged into his room, packed up Sam's stuff, and quietly left Power Academy. I had a hunch before that something wasn't right, and that just confirmed it.

When I wasn't rehearsing, working with Sabrina, or in the middle of class, Sam was all I thought about.

We were in rehearsal now. The magical fairies were situated center stage in the middle of a forest. Huge green and yellow paper trees stood at least seven feet high. The Wednesdays were backstage, attempting to get the strings of lights wrapped around the huge props to glow. Tiny eleven-year-old Lester Manchester, Sam's mentee, was the only Wednesday to have any success—he lit one single bulb. The rest of the powerless Wednesdays? Nada.

I watched as Lester turned toward Mr. Fluxnut to ask, "And will he be coming back?" Of course, he was asking about Sam.

"He had to leave due to an unexpected family issue, so I'm not sure how long it will be," Mr. Fluxnut said robotically. For a drama teacher, he could have at least *acted* concerned.

Why wouldn't he have told us about an "unexpected issue"?

"Now, how are we supposed to have an enchanted forest when you Wednesdays can't even do your part?" Mr. Fluxnut yelled, walking away from Lester and across the stage, flicking the rest of the lights on himself.

"Continue," he yelled. "Let's go, Poppy! Hustle, hustle, please!"

I entered stage right while the other Monday fairies swarmed around me, and read, "How now, spirit? Whither wander you?"

Sabrina, who was playing Fairy One, responded, "Over hill, over dale, Thorough bush, thorough brier, Over park, over pale, Through …"

Sabrina hesitated. She didn't know her next line.

"Uh … um … uh …" she stuttered.

"Book!" Mr. Fluxnut yelled.

In a flick of my wrist, I telekinetically lifted a script from the front of the stage and into the hands of Sabrina.

She frowned. "I'll never get this," she said, reading over her lines.

Mr. Fluxnut rested his elbows on the edge of the stage and spoke. "It's really not that difficult to remember a few measly lines. I knew I gave you a minor role for a reason," he said through tight lips.

I could see tears begin to form in the corners of Sabrina's eyes and rested my hand on her shoulder. She brushed the teardrops away with the back of her hand.

Mr. Fluxnut jumped up on stage and stood so close to Sabrina that only she and I could hear. Unless, of course, you were a mind-reading Thursday.

"If your Monday power is as weak as your memorization

skills, then you might as well be a Sunday, just like your mother," Mr. Fluxnut continued through gritted teeth, staring Sabrina straight in the eyes.

"I … I … um …" she mumbled, running off stage, with sobs escaping from her lips. I followed after her.

"Not cool," I yelled at Mr. Fluxnut as I jumped off the stage. I followed Sabrina down the backstage stairs to the dressing room area. "Continue, everyone!" Mr. Fluxnut's voice cut through the air. Obviously, he didn't care about the fact he just ran a poor little powerless Monday offstage.

I got to the bottom of the stairs just as the dressing room door slammed in my face. I knocked gently three times. "Sabrina? Can I come in?"

Silence.

"It's me … Poppy."

"Leave me alone," she responded through sobs. I didn't have to read her mind to know she was embarrassed and upset by what had just occurred.

"Is she okay?" Logan asked, placing a hand on my shoulder.

"Please, I just want to talk to you," I pleaded toward the door.

I turned to face Logan. "Just focus on Lester and Deklan right now," I whispered to him. "I need to deal with this alone." I grabbed his hand and squeezed it.

Is everything okay? I heard Ellie ask in my head.

I'll be up soon, I thought back to her.

I knocked again. "Please," I asked one more time, now resting my head on the wooden door. I was just beginning to know Sabrina, and already she seemed defeated. Mr. Fluxnut just made it even worse. It was my job to help her master her Monday power, so I wasn't about to give up. That's just not what a Mayberry does.

Creak. Sabrina's bright blue eyes peeked out. "Is anyone else out there?"

"Just me." I smiled.

"I'm just having a tough time with this …" she paused and rolled her eyes. "*All* of this."

She didn't have to say anything more. The pressure of mastering her Monday power was difficult enough, but now she also had to perform in front of an audience—in less than two weeks—in a play directed by the weirdest, meanest man ever.

"I know this seems tough," I said, even though Sabrina's challenge to memorize a few lines was nothing compared to the challenge Ellie, Logan, Sam, and I had last summer.

"But it feels just as hard as your challenge was," she said, responding to the comment I just made. In my head.

My body went stiff.

"I never said that aloud," I whispered to her.

She shrugged and sat down in a chair, hands on her head. "I wanted to tell you before, Poppy."

Tell me what? I thought, testing her.

"That I'm not *just* a Monday," she said matter-of-factly.

Sabrina was just like me. I knew it for sure. I also knew that her mom was a powerless weekend and her dad was a Tuesday, and to be a cusper, your cusp power had to match the power of one of your parents. So how could that even happen? It didn't make sense.

I sat down in the chair across from her. "When did you know you had two powers?"

Before she could answer though, there was a knock on the door. "What's going on in here?" Headmistress Larriby asked, wedging through the half-open door.

"We're just finishing up," I answered. I brushed a strand of frilly red hair from my face and stood up. "She just came down with a small case of stage fright," I said nonchalantly. By the look on Larriby's face, she bought my lie. I hoped she couldn't see my shaking hands.

"Come on," I said, grabbing Sabrina's hand. "Let's get back up there."

There was still so much I needed to learn about the

whole cusp power thing. If a girl with a powerless Sunday mother and a teleporting Tuesday father was a cusper, then there was more to these cusp powers than I thought. Somebody wasn't telling the whole truth.

Chapter Thirteen

I walked up to my room to let Pickle wander around a bit before meeting up with Logan and Ellie to fill them in on the Sabrina situation. Together, we would all be able to figure it out. It was just so strange that someone with a Thursday cusp power, without a parent who's a Thursday, could actually be a ... well ... Thursday.

I fumbled with the giant purple headpiece in my hand—the prop I'd be wearing during the performance— as I attempted to get a good grasp of my room key to unlock the door. That wasn't going well, so I used my Monday power to suspend the headpiece in air, but just as I rounded the corner of the hallway, my telekinetic thought flew from my head and the purple and sparkle-embellished prop crashed to the wooden planks below my feet. Someone I didn't expect to see was waiting outside my room—Veronica.

The key dropped from my other hand as we rushed to hug one another.

"I'm sorry," she said. I wasn't sure if she said it aloud or in her head, but I knew that she meant it either way.

"I'm sorry," I said right back.

We pulled away from each other and smiled.

"I just—" we spoke at the same time.

"You go," I said.

"I have to tell you something that really can't wait." She looked left and then right, her eyes shifting nervously up and down the hallway.

"Come on," I said, "let's get inside."

We entered my room to see Ellie propped up on her bed, reading.

"Huh," Veronica sighed.

I knew Ellie was the last person she wanted to see, but I wasn't about to kick my roommate out of her own room. Plus, Ellie and Veronica were both my friends, and it was about time they became comfortable with each other.

"Hey, Veronica," Ellie perked up. She lifted her pointer

finger toward the dresser drawer.

"Uhh … hmm," I gruffed, hoping she would catch my hint.

Her finger shot back to her side and she used her hands to place the magazine back in her nightstand. Even if someone else knew about my cusp power, I wasn't ready for Veronica to see that she shared Monday with Ellie, as well. That was an invitation for even more jealousy.

"So what was it you wanted to tell me?" I asked Veronica, trying to draw her attention away from the faux pas Ellie almost made.

"Does *she* have to be here?" Veronica whispered, gesturing toward Ellie.

I had to make a decision. And quick. Either I let Ellie stay, making Veronica upset yet again. Or I tell Ellie to leave, which would make her upset with me. Ugh. Why did Veronica have to put me in this position?

I looked at Veronica, and then Ellie, and then back at Veronica and shrugged.

"I can take a hint," Ellie said, grabbing her magazine from the nightstand and stomping out of the room. She obviously read my mind.

Once the door slammed behind her I spoke. "Seriously? Do you have to be so rude?" It seemed that our conversations always came back to this. To Ellie. To Veronica's jealousy.

Veronica plopped herself down on Ellie's bed and sighed. "Look, I didn't come here to argue with you. I just need to fill you in on some things and then you can go back to your," she nodded toward the door, "friend."

"Did you get my letter?" I asked hopefully, trying to show her that I cared about her. About our friendship.

The corners of Veronica's mouth turned up slightly. "Yes. Thank you. Logan dropped it off."

But that's not why she was here. I could sense that.

"I thought it better to talk to you in person rather than write back," she paused and glanced down to her lap. "This is something that I need to say face-to-face. Especially considering the weird things you mentioned in the letter."

"What a sec," I said, just realizing something. "How did you get here, anyway?"

Veronica sat down on Ellie's bed and Pickle hopped up next to her. Veronica's eyes darted up and to the room's four corners. "There aren't, like, any cameras or anything in here, right?" she asked.

"No, not that I know of," I replied. She was scaring me.

Veronica leaned in closer to me. "I got a ride with your dad." She shrugged her shoulders.

"I know there's more to the story than that," I said.

"Well, he didn't actually *know* I was in the car. Before he left for work this morning, I simply got in the back of his car, hid under a blanket, and then hopped out once he got in the N.P.C. building."

"That is so something you'd see on television!" I said, shocked that Veronica could pull it off.

"Right? Don't you think it's weird that we have to be so sneaky about everything in this town?"

I nodded. Veronica was right. We weren't allowed to use our weekday powers outside of Nova, let alone step foot outside of our town. I couldn't tell anyone about my cusp power. Nobody knew where my friend Sam went, and nobody was talking about it. And we can't even get visitors at Power Academy. "Yes. There's no reason why you shouldn't be able to visit Power Academy any time you want to."

"I heard something I need you to know." Veronica took a breath and began. "So yesterday, I stopped by your house to drop off those three headbands I borrowed a few weeks ago." I remembered. Veronica's cousin got married and Veronica had narrowed her outfits down to three— one red, one pink, and one purple. I have a headband to match every outfit I own, so naturally she came to me to accessorize.

"Anyway, your mom and dad told me just to take them up to your room. So I did. And I did it fast."

"Okay …"

"But they must not have heard me coming back down the stairs because I heard them whispering about something in the kitchen." She scooted closer to me.

"What does this have to do with weird stuff in my letter?"

Veronica rolled her eyes. "I'm getting there."

"Okay."

"Well, your dad's worked at Nova Power Corporation for what, like 20 years, right?"

"Yeah. So?" I wished she would get to the point.

"I heard him bring up a couple names of weekdays going missing over the last two years or so. He mentioned a name I didn't recognize, so I just brushed it off. I mean, sometimes people just go missing. Runaways, moving, stuff like that."

I nodded, leaning closer to her.

"But then he said Sam's name, and that's when I really started to listen." Veronica pointed toward the door. I knew she was double-checking to see that it was closed.

"Poppy, Sam isn't like the rest of us," she whispered so quietly I could barely hear. This would be the perfect time to tell her about my secret. *Should I?* I thought.

"What do you mean?" I asked, sensing her answer was something I was all too familiar with.

"Your dad called him something. A cusper, I think it was." Her eyes grew wide. "Sam has double the power of a regular Wednesday."

"Wow," I said, feigning surprise. How much did she really hear? "But how?"

"I don't know, but these cuspers can have double their power or the powers of *two* weekdays."

I swallowed, thinking about poor Sam, wherever he was now, and knowing what she was about to say.

"And they're disappearing, Poppy. I heard your dad say it. They're disappearing, and no one, not even your dad, can figure where they're going."

I tried to wrap my head around what Veronica had just said. People were going missing. Not just any people. Cuspers. I swallowed hard, knowing I could very well be next the next one.

Chapter Fourteen

Last year, if you'd asked me if I wanted to have two powers, I'm not sure how I would have answered. Really, I had just wanted to be good at one. And if I knew two powers would be dangerous to me, then I definitely wouldn't have wanted them.

Ellie, Logan, and I sat in Headmistress Larriby's office, waiting for her. She didn't know we were here. She hadn't bothered to change the combination on the lock from last year, so we simply typed it in and voila. No need to use powers of any sort.

Last year's challenge was a way for us to not only prove our powers, but also to realize our true potential as cuspers.

As much as I wanted to believe that the disappearances of Sam and the other cuspers was another challenge, I had a bad feeling about it. This wasn't just something concocted in the strange minds of Larriby and Grimeley. We weren't playing with missing jewelry, athletic equipment, musical instruments, and dogs. Human lives were at stake this time.

The doorknob turned slowly.

"What the—" Mrs. Larriby said, obviously taken aback by our appearance in her office.

She sighed. "I know why you're here," she said, taking a seat behind her desk. *You just can't let that thing with Mark Masters go, can you?* she thought to me, her eyes burning into me so hard that I thought I would catch fire right then and there.

"There is something strange happening here, and we want to know what," I said matter-of-factly.

"And we don't plan on leaving unless you tell us," Logan chimed in.

"Hmmm," Larriby sighed, giving us the same nervous look she did when Mr. Fluxnut entered the room on the first day of camp. He had told her something that frightened her, and I had a feeling that she was about to tell us. I used my Thursday power. *Should I or not?*

"I feel like we need to know what's going on," Ellie said,

gingerly, and innocently batted her eyelashes. "First that thing with Mark, which Poppy obviously told us about." Headmistress Larriby scowled at me. Ellie continued, "And then Sam disappears. And then Veronica show—" Ellie paused, her eyes meeting mine. "I mean, we just want to know what's going on."

Beads of sweat began to form on Larriby's brow. She looked terrified. She scooted her seat into the desk and leaned toward us.

"Okay," she said, puffing out a lungful of air. She made up her mind to tell us. "You really should know because it has *everything* to do with you."

Ellie's arm lifted and pointed to the office door. It slammed shut.

"Someone's doing something with some of the cuspers," Headmistress Larriby whispered.

"Excuse me? What?" Ellie demanded.

"Well, we're not entirely sure what is happening. Let's just say, for a bit of time, some cuspers have ... well, just be careful," she said, without finishing her original sentence. Luckily, my Thursday power was now strong enough to read from her mind what she wanted to say: *vanished.*

"What do you mean, vanished?" Ellie asked, obviously reading Larriby's mind, too.

Larriby sighed. "I'm sorry to be telling you this but, yet again, I haven't been completely honest with you all."

"No kidding," Logan mumbled. "When are you ever honest with us?"

Silence.

Headmistress Larriby tapped her pointer finger on the table in front of her. "Part of the reason you're at Power Academy this summer is to help the weekdays become proficient in their given powers. That is the truth. But we have you here for another reason as well."

"Who's the we?" Ellie asked. I also wanted to know the answer.

"Mayor Masters and I, of course."

Of course. That made sense. That's probably why Mayor Masters has been checking on us these last few days.

"Due to the missing cuspers, Mayor Masters felt it was in your best interest to stay here under the pretense of camp counselors." She paused, and pulled a file from her top desk drawer. "And until we find who's behind this, you are here." She shifted the folder to the other hand. "For your own safety."

She slapped the folder down on her desk.

"How safe are we, really? I mean, Sam disappeared. And I don't even know what was going on with Mark. And you're trying to tell us that being here is *in our best interest*?" Logan asked, making air quotes with his fingers.

He was right. I didn't feel any safer here than I would in my own home.

"Look. People here and at the N.P.C. are trying to get to the bottom of this, but until then, you're staying put." She stood up and placed her hands firmly on the table. "That decision's already been made."

"But what about our par—" Ellie started.

Clothes-too-tight Larriby opened the folder in front of her. "Your parents are in complete agreement with this decision. Even they believe it best you are here under our supervision."

In the folder were four documents. Larriby's sausage-like fingers slid a sheet to each of us.

"Permission slips," Ellie acknowledged, sighing.

At the bottom of the page were the cursive signatures of my mom and dad. They did, indeed, know about the cusper situation, and they'd given their permission for us to stay here under false pretenses. Why hadn't mom told me before I left? This was so not okay.

Larriby's voice brought my attention back to her. "As I said, those at Nova Power Corporation are looking into this right now. In fact, that is top priority. There are agents placed all over Nova keeping an eye on cuspers like you." I slid the paper back to her side of the table.

I thought back to my first sighting of Mr. Fluxnut at Novalicious; I bet that's why he was there that day. He wasn't watching me because he was a total creeper. He was watching me for protection. He was looking out for me. And Mayor Masters checked up on us for our own good, our own protection.

"But why didn't you just tell us, then? Instead of tricking us?" Logan asked, pushing the sheet of paper back to Larriby.

"We simply didn't want to alarm you." She cleared her throat. "Those at N.P.C. are still trying to grasp the cusper ability, and until things are more solidified, we didn't want to bring unneeded attention to individuals like you."

"But Sam is missing, so how protected are we here?" Ellie said. Her voice shook as she spoke. She was afraid, and I couldn't blame her. Larriby just confirmed it—cuspers were disappearing, and not even the higher-ups at Nova Power Corporation knew where they were going.

"That was an unfortunate oversight, and the N.P.C. is doing everything in its power to find Sam." Larriby's eyes softened, exposing another new side to her. "We will find him," she said, now looking at Ellie, who sniffed back tears.

It seemed like Headmistress Larriby was reassuring herself.

If we wanted to find Sam, I had a feeling that we would have to do it ourselves, but I didn't even know where to begin.

Chapter Fifteen

I decided to put the whole disappearing cusper situation out of my mind as best as I could. It was beyond my control at this point, and we were assured that N.P.C. was on it. We just needed to let them do their jobs so we could focus on ours—getting our mentees weekday ready. Easier said than done.

I walked into Monday power intensive class the next morning and was happily greeted by Sabrina. "Hey, Poppy!" she said, beaming. "Something amazing happened last night. Watch." Her enthusiasm was contagious and a nice distraction from my worries.

I smiled. "Okay. Go ahead."

Sabrina lifted her left hand and pointed toward the back of the room. *Slide. Slide. Slide,* she willed the chair in the back corner.

I stared at the chair, but it didn't budge. I thought about sliding it using my own Monday power, just to give her a boost of confidence, but decided that that wouldn't be the best idea. It was my job to see that she mastered her power, not to do the hard work for her.

Slide. Slide. Slide, she said in her head with more force. And just when I was about to give up on her, the chair began to wobble.

Now! she thought. Faster than my eyes could follow, the chair slid sharply to the right, smacking into Hunter. He swayed back and forth on his feet and then fell to the floor.

"Oh my gosh. Hunter? I am so sorry!" Sabrina ran up to him and tugged on his arm.

"Nah. Don't worry about it," he said, swiping bits of dirt from his pants.

"That's amazing, Sabrina!" I said, hugging her. "I'm so proud of you!"

And I really was. This was huge for Sabrina, and I was happy to be her mentor. Over the past few days, we had been fitting in mini-lessons over lunch, after rehearsals, and during any downtime. It seemed that our hard work had paid off.

"I can't wait to show Miss Maggie!" she said excitedly, getting out her notebook and pen. "I'm ready for whatever assignment we get today."

I debated whether or not to tell her that I had a bunch of ups and downs with my Monday power before I totally controlled it, but decided against it. "That really is amazing," I said, a grin spreading across my face.

Miss Maggie entered the classroom and used her Monday power to shut the door. A breeze flew through my hair, pushing a few spirally red curls in my eyes. I suddenly wished I had thrown it up in a messy bun this morning.

Today, Miss Maggie had on a vibrant pink skirt with a white top and a blue necklace that jingled with each step she took. I wished that I'll have her sense of style when I got older—posh with a hint of casualness. When she opened her mouth and the British accent came out, her chicness grew even more.

"Today we have a special guest with us," she said. I followed her gaze to the back of the room where her mother, Mayor Masters stood. Mayor Masters had a ginormous smile on her face—she was obviously proud of her daughter.

"Mayor Masters is just popping into the classrooms today to see what exactly it is we do in the summer program."

"Yes," Mayor Masters said. "I just love seeing the progress weekday students make over a few short weeks. Even if you're behind in your powers, it's good to know you aren't a Saturday or Sunday," she said through a forced chuckle.

Then I thought of her powerless son, Mark. Poor kid. Still, after hearing the news of cuspers going missing, being a powerless weekend didn't sound so bad.

Miss Maggie began her lesson. "Today, we will be talking about breaking barriers with our Monday powers." Her eyes met mine for a split second before she continued. "Sometimes, we will encounter instances when we need to harness more power than usual." Today, her typical smile was replaced with a stoic expression. Something was up. Maybe her mother told her about the missing students. That would make anyone feel pretty bummed.

She walked to the back of the room and, using her Monday power, slid the bookshelf from the wall to reveal the secret compartment I knew was there.

Last year, the hidden compartment's shelves were filled with candies, chocolate, and sweet goodies of all sorts.

When she slid the case over this time, the shelves were empty. I wasn't sure what this had to do with today's lesson, but I was positive all would reveal itself shortly.

"If you ever find yourself in harm's way, it's important to know that you can use your power for escape." She said this without any expression. Yes, something was definitely off with Miss Maggie.

With three effortless flicks of her wrist, a gust of wind escaped from the tips of her fingers and sharply hit the three shelves in the wall. All three pieces of wood cracked and then crumbled to the ground in a pile of debris. We all stared at the shelfless wall and clapped.

"Did she just do that, for real?" an awestruck Morgan asked.

"That was amazing," Caleb added.

Even I, a pretty powerful Monday, was in awe. I'd seen Mondays move pretty heavy and cumbersome objects. Heck, I'd cracked a few wooden planks last year when I broke into the old shed to rescue Pickle. But I'd never seen anyone crumble multiple pieces of wood at once.

"Now, watch closely once again," she said, her last word rhyming with *mane*. I never got tired of her British accent. "Poppy, you help this time."

I mimicked her movement and lifted my arm.

"On three," she said. "One. Two. Three!"

After three quick flicks of our wrists, the exposed wall that was situated behind the now-destroyed shelves cracked right down the middle. Miss Maggie flicked her wrist one more time and a few smaller cracks appeared around the original. Not two seconds later, pieces of wall crumbled down on top of the destroyed shelves. There was now a gaping hole in the middle of the hidden closet. Simply amazing.

"No way!" Sabrina shouted. She bent over, poked her head through the hole and then looked at me. "You can see into the next room!" Her eyes grew wide.

With a few more wrist movements, the crumbled pieces of wall and shelves came back together in perfect form. Gasps escaped from the mouths of the Mondays.

"Now back to your seats, ladies and gentleman," Miss Maggie announced. Everyone did as they were told.

"Never underestimate the powers of those around you. It's important to realize that although you've been gifted with an amazing ability, with that ability comes the power to destroy. Never forget that." Maggie looked briefly to the back of the room and then cracked the first smile I saw from her today. I turned around to see Mayor Masters leaving the room in a rush.

"That's a weird thing to say," Sabrina whispered, nudging my shoulder.

"Mm-hmm," I nodded. And that's when I realized that, just like last year, Miss Maggie had created this lesson for a reason. But I wasn't so sure what it was.

Chapter Sixteen

Another day went by without so much as a word of the missing cuspers, except, of course, when Logan, Ellie, and I ate together. Last night at dinner, Ellie couldn't stop herself from crying. She felt betrayed by her family, scared for Sam, and scared for herself. The three of us all felt terrified in general. If what Headmistress Larriby and Veronica said was one-hundred-percent true, then there was a chance that we could go missing too. There is no way we could let that happen.

I had to trust Headmistress Larriby and her insistence that we were, indeed, safe here. My task today was to help Sabrina master her Monday power.

Sabrina got better and better every time I saw her, which was hard to believe considering we'd only been here for a week. She was so good, in fact, that I forgot that she could also read minds. But she was doing it the right way—mastering one power at a time. I wondered if Headmistress Larriby knew that Sabrina was a Thursday, too. After all, she had said that there were no cusp students at Power Academy this year. Why would she lie? I was starting to believe that Veronica was on to something when she mentioned all the secrets hidden in Nova. It was like telling the truth actually hurt people in this town.

"It might be a good idea not to mention the dual power thing to anyone," I had said to Sabrina yesterday at the afternoon power intensive class.

"Why?" she had asked.

I didn't want to frighten her with the knowledge of cuspers disappearing, so I decided to tell her another truth. "Your second power will come in easier if you've already mastered your first one."

I looked up at the mirror in front of me now. My bright orange hair was pulled up in two purple cones, and hair was pom-poming from the tops of the shiny cylinders. I would never choose to wear the purple leotard with the sparkly overlay that fit like a glove, but the costume designer,

Emily, said that there wasn't a better color to complement my orange hair and green eyes.

"Your eyes look pretty," Logan said, as if he had read my mind. Which I knew he totally didn't.

"Thanks," I said, and reached my hands up to my cheeks and pinched. A light pink hue spread across my face. Logan twisted his mouth up in confusion. "For color," I said to him, our eyes meeting through the mirror's reflection. Maybe I was just covering up the fact that he had just made me blush.

Out of nowhere, he reached down and grabbed my hand. "You'll be great," he said, sensing my anxiety. It was only a rehearsal, but I was a bundle of nerves. I was not a performer. Then unexpectedly, Logan pulled me up from the chair and wrapped both arms around me. Now I really didn't want him to look at me—I was sure my face was beet red.

He pulled his face closer to mine, reminding me of the end of Power Academy last year when he kissed me on the cheek. I got nervous but for no reason—he didn't kiss me this time.

"Poppy!" The sound of Sabrina's voice pushed us apart.

"I'll see you out there," Logan said with a warm smile and hand-squeeze as he made his way out of the dressing room.

"I need to talk to you about something," Sabrina said, following me toward the stage.

"What's up?" I said, trying to sound chipper. She was my mentee, so my stage fright was the last thing I needed her to see.

"Places!" I heard Ellie yell.

"I know we have to start, but I have to talk to you."

"I'm sorry, Mr. Fluxnut will kill me if I'm not in place." I turned to look at her face-to-face. She frowned.

"You know how he gets."

In a hushed voice she said, "We *need* to talk later. The N.P.C. … and Mark." Cara Flohr, the stage manager, pushed herself between us, but Sabrina continued. "I read her mind," she paused, "We can't trust—" Sabrina's words came out in short, random phrases. She just couldn't get a hold of her words.

"Places!" Ellie yelled one final time, cutting Sabrina off from whatever she was trying to tell me. As an assistant stage-managing Thursday pushed me toward my opening position, I attempted to read Sabrina's mind, but there were too many people running to their places and shouting last-minute stage directions to get a good grasp.

Whatever Sabrina had to tell me had to wait until later. Now, I stood behind the giant red curtain and took two big breaths as she disappeared off in the wings, awaiting her entrance.

"In three. Two," Logan called, and shot me a quick wink. He thought this would help overcome my stage fright, but it just reminded me that I would be performing in front of a huge audience at the end of the Power Academy summer session. "One."

I was so not getting used to being on stage. I felt butterflies flit around in my stomach as the curtain began to rise, knowing this was silly considering it was only a rehearsal, but when those lights shine in your eyes, it's hard to forget you're on stage.

I stepped to center stage and began. "A magic carpet, friends, I'll weave for you. Of slender moonbeams and of silver dew. I'll spread it out before your feet, and lo, Swift as the wind through time and space we go."

That was Sabrina's cue to enter stage right. Using her Monday power, she was supposed to make paper machete butterflies flutter around us while reciting her opening line. But she didn't enter.

I repeated my opening two lines, thinking that, perhaps, she didn't hear the first time. I began, my voice louder, yet shakier, this time. "A magic carpet, friends, I'll weave for you. Of slender moonbeams and of silver dew. I'll spread it out before your feet, and lo, Swift as the wind through time and space we go."

Again, nothing. No Sabrina. This was unusual. The last two rehearsals, she not only seemed to have her stage fright under control, but actually became extra confident because she'd started to get the hang of her Monday power. There was no reason for her to flake out now.

"Sabrina," Mr. Fluxnut called. His voice grew more impatient. "Sabrina!" he yelled and stomped his way toward the stage. "Sabrina!" he screamed again. His face started to turn as purple as the too-clingy fabric of my costume.

There was still no sign of the petite Monday.

Ellie, I thought to Ellie. *Go check the dressing room.* Ellie didn't make her grand entrance until scene three, so I knew that she had time to check.

A few seconds later, Ellie responded in my head. "No luck here."

"This is absolutely ridiculous," Mr. Fluxnut said. "Where is she?"

Where did she go? I just talked to her a few seconds ago. She was in her spritely sparkly peach costume, and now she was nowhere to be found.

Suddenly, I knew exactly why. She was a cusper, even if not everyone knew she was one. And just like Sam, Sabrina had disappeared too.

Chapter Seventeen

"Look. I know something weird is going on at N.P.C, so I think that's where we need to go," I said, pushing the tray of grossness away from me. I looked down at the dog food-like stuffing sitting on my plate. Why do they even feed this to us? Up until now, the food has been awesome this year. I stared at the gray-brown blob in front of me and gagged. Seriously, it looked like something Pickle would eat.

I glanced up at Logan, who was shoving forkfuls in his face. At least one of us was enjoying it.

"How do we even get into N.P.C.?" Ellie asked.

I looked around to make sure nobody was listening in.

Deklan and Shelby were still in the extraordinarily long food line, so it would be at least another fifteen minutes until they joined us.

Headmistress Larriby was on the other side of the cafeteria in deep conversation with Mayor Masters, their eyes frantically looking around from time to time. Last year, Headmistress Larriby's eyes would have been glaring right in our direction, but whatever was happening this year went way beyond us.

We all leaned in closer to one another. "Right before I went on stage at rehearsal today, Sabrina tried to tell me something. And she mentioned two things that I think go together—Nova Power Corporation and Mark Masters."

I glanced back over at Mayor Masters—she was still talking to Larriby, and whenever she paused and looked around the room, a smile formed on her face. How could she be so happy when people were missing? Then I realized that she probably painted that smile so the students wouldn't be alarmed.

"But you said it yourself, Poppy," Logan said, taking a bite of food. "N.P.C. is a fortress. How would we even get in without being seen?"

"Do I even have to say it?"

As if he read my mind, he answered. "No way!" He

shook his head. "If I get caught in that place, who knows what they would do to me?"

We'd all heard the horror stories of weekdays breaking into Nova Power Corporation at its old location, never to be seen again. My dad said that was totally untrue, and I believe everything he says.

But I'd forgotten that teleporting wasn't even an option for Logan anyway. Teleporting Tuesdays could only use their powers to teleport to places they'd been before. Since Logan had never even stepped foot in Nova Power Corporation, that wasn't going to happen.

"And what could we do, anyway?" Ellie said. "We don't even know what we'd be looking for."

"Uhhh … Sam," I said, rolling my eyes. "Duh. And Sabrina."

"And why do you think they would be there? They went missing. You heard Mayor Masters. N.P.C. is looking for them right now."

As much as I wanted to believe N.P.C. was looking for them, I had a feeling that wasn't the case. I imagined poor Sam and his big cowboy hat. And little, frightened Sabrina. She barely had control over her powers, so how was she going to survive?

Ellie pushed pieces of broccoli around with a fork. It

was very unlike her not to eat veggies, so she was obviously distraught. I knew she wouldn't admit it, but she definitely had a crush on Sam.

I do not, she thought.

I smiled. *We'll find him*, I thought right back.

"I don't know," said Ellie. "But we have other important things to think about."

Like what, I thought. People were disappearing, and we could be the next ones. What was more important than that?

"The play!" Ellie said enthusiastically, suddenly perking up. At least she could take her mind off of the craziness that is Power Academy.

"Two of the actors have disappeared. How will the play even go on?" Logan asked.

"Oh, Mr. Fluxnut already found replacements, silly! Isn't that exciting?"

"Yeah, Ellie," I said unenthused. "Just about as exciting as this delicious meal here." Using my Monday power, I used my spoon to pick up a blob of brown stuffing before plopping it back down on the plate. I remembered back to last summer when I tried to do the same thing. It didn't go so well then—much of it had ended up on Ellie.

"Oh, come on, Poppy. You need to perk up. Maybe we

should do a little warm-up exercise?" Ellie bent her elbows, placed her hands under her armpits, and started flapping away. I cracked a smile.

"There you go!" she exclaimed. "That's the Poppy I like to see."

Logan chuckled along. It felt good to laugh a bit, especially considering what we were dealing with. One by one, cuspers were disappearing and we had no clue if we'd be next.

"Sorry, Poppy," Ellie said. I knew she was trying to lighten the mood, but she knew, just as we all did, that there was something strange going on with N.P.C. and Power Academy. Something that we would have to figure out because it was clear that Headmistress Larriby had no clue what to do about it. From here on out, we had to constantly be looking over our shoulders.

"Can we please decide what exactly we're going to do, though?" I asked, bringing us back on task. "I just have a feeling they're close by. Clothes-too-tight Larriby explained what was going on with the cuspers, but she never even mentioned if it was connected to Mark Masters."

"That's true. She never even brought him up at all."

I leaned in and whispered, "I know we have no proof, but I just have this gut feeling that Mark has something to do with the missing cuspers. These things have to be connected, especially after what Sabrina said right before she …" I couldn't finish the thought. Last year, my gut didn't mislead me when Pickle went missing, and I knew it wasn't misleading me this year.

"What if Mark's a secret cusper too, and that whole Saturday talk is just a lie?" Logan offered. "Or," Logan said, looking right into my eyes, "maybe we should ask your dad. I mean, he does work at N.P.C."

I shook my head. "No way. He's not even allowed to talk about his job to my mom. It's like, super security stuff." And again—all the Nova secrets. "How did they even know that Sabrina was a cusper?" I added. "I mean, with her parents being the days that they are, that just doesn't make any sense." I used my Monday power to slide the fruit cup from Logan's tray to mine—I knew he wouldn't eat it, and I'd suddenly realized how hungry I was.

He smiled at me as a few strands of hair fell over his eyes. My cheeks grew warm as I sent a rush of wind his way to push them back in place.

Thanks, he thought.

"That's why we need to get into N.P.C.," Logan said in a hushed voice. "Obviously, they know things that we don't, and I have a feeling that this is one of those things."

He was on board. Now we just needed Ellie.

She smiled. "Well, what are we waiting for, then?" Ellie said, taking me off guard. "Let's do it," she added, just as her and Logan's mentees sat down next to us.

Later that evening, Ellie, Logan, and I sneaked through the administration hallway to the internal entrance of Nova Power Corporation, where I had seen Mark Masters at the beginning of the Power Academy summer program. Gosh, so much had changed in just a few days. We studied the little blinking black box on the side of the door, but just couldn't figure it out.

"What we need is Sam," Logan said matter-of-factly. Ellie frowned, and I could tell by the pouty lips that she was holding back tears. She had gushed non-stop this past school year about spending the first few weeks of the summer with Sam, and now that he was missing, I could tell she was totally bummed. Beyond bummed—she was upset and sad. We all were.

Logan was right. Where a normal Wednesday's

electricity-manipulating power couldn't break through a high-tech door like this one, Sam's double Wednesday may actually be able to. But he wasn't here, and that was the reason we were breaking into N.P.C. in the first place. Well, Sam and Sabrina. And Mark—I wasn't sure why, but he definitely needed our help, too. That whole internship-with-maintenance thing was so not the truth.

I took another look at Headmistress Larriby's office door. We had tried her code a number of times, but it hadn't worked. In fact, we had attempted every four-digit combination we could think of that somehow related to Nova— the first day the meteor struck, the day Roy Lichtenstein discovered his power, the day N.P.C. was created—and nothing. This was so frustrating. If only it were as easy as last year.

And then it came to me. It might be as easy as last year, and with the right equipment, maybe even easier.

"Swipe card," I said, looking to the left of the keypad at the place where a thin access card could be swiped.

"Huh?" Ellie asked.

"We need a swipe card."

"Okay …"

Logan caught the hint. "Your dad," he said, his jaw dropped.

Taking a cue from Ellie, I batted my eyelashes. "I need a huge favor," I said to Logan.

He squinted. "Uh … Poppy? What's wrong with your eye?"

Apparently I was batting them a little too hard.

"Oh … just an eyelash." I fake-pulled an eyelash from my eye and said, "Better."

Flirting wasn't my thing, so I cut to the chase. "So, I was wondering if you could do another favor for me?" I asked in my sweetest Poppy voice.

"Anything. You know that, Poppy," Logan said, leaning in closer to me. My mind flashed back to that kiss on the cheek and I blushed. Was it wrong that I wanted another one now?

"You need to get that card from my dad."

"But how?" he asked, leaning back into his original position.

"Teleport, of course."

"But what about the whole can't-teleport-to-a-place-you've-never-been-before thing?" Ellie interjected.

"Logan left his swim towel at your house, so I took it home with me at the end of last summer," I said. "He had to stop by to pick it up." I looked at Logan. "So, will you do it?"

Silence. "I really don't want my first encounter with your dad to be me stealing his I.D. card," he said.

"Well, what did you want it to be like then?" I said, suddenly hoping he would invite himself over for dinner, or lunch, or for any reason, really.

"I don't know. Anything except him waking up to find a stranger creeping around his house in the middle of the night. And he'd be all like, 'who are you?' And I'd be like, 'Hey, I'm Logan. Poppy's boy ... uh ... friend.'"

We laughed. "True. But you know as well as I do that you'll never get caught." It was simple; he would teleport there and then do the disappearing Friday thing to snatch my dad's access badge. "You'll do it, right?" I said, taking a step forward and lessening the empty space between us.

It didn't take much for him to give in. "Sure."

"Okay then," I said. I don't know what compelled me to do it, but then I stood up on my tiptoes and kissed *him* on the cheek.

Three things happened at once. Logan smiled. I stepped down. Ellie's jaw practically fell to the floor. I pivoted so they couldn't see the huge smile that spread across my face.

"Let's meet at the same place, same time tomorrow night," I yelled as I made my way back to our room.

Chapter Eighteen

A few other students had noticed that Sam and Sabrina went missing, and Lester asked Mr. Fluxnut about it the next day after rehearsal.

"Sam had to go home due to a family emergency, and Sabrina had no hope with her Monday power, so we dismissed her before she embarrassed herself even further," Mr. Fluxnut had explained to us all, even though it was obvious Sabrina was Mondaying-it-up all over the place. I couldn't have been the only one to notice that.

"Oh," was all the others muttered. They seemed to believe those ridiculous responses. They were too busy trying to master their own powers to even notice Fluxnut's shoddy coverup. Something was off with that guy.

Now, it was dark in Power Academy, and all the other weekdays were fast asleep in their dorm rooms. Ellie and I were in our room, counting down the minutes until we were to meet Logan back at the N.P.C. entrance.

"Why do we even need to stay? If Sam and Sabrina went missing from Power Academy—where they were supposed to be safe—how is being home more dangerous?" Ellie asked, pacing the room and then finally sitting on the edge of her bed. We had rehashed this same topic over and over again and couldn't quite figure it out. We were supposed to be safe here, but the fact that cuspers were disappearing so close to N.P.C. made it seem more logical that they were being held there. If this plan didn't work, I would be going home tomorrow.

Just like during last year's mission, Ellie was dressed from head to toe in black camouflage. Even her nails were painted midnight black. Last year I rolled my eyes at this, but now I was used to it. My lips curled into a smile as I thought back to how far we'd come in our friendship.

With a flick of her wrist, Ellie sent the bottle of dark liquid flying in my direction. Using my Monday power, I swiped one coat of paint on my nails as well. Might as well break the rules in style.

"It's almost time," Ellie said, pushing herself from the bed.

"I hope he comes through," I said, absentmindedly dropping the bottle of nail polish in my pocket.

When we got to the end of the administration hallway a few minutes later, there was no sign of Logan.

"What if your dad found him wandering around your house?" Ellie asked. I didn't want to think of what that could mean. Would he call the Nova police? Or worse—escort him back to Power Academy himself? I could only imagine Headmistress Larriby's reaction when she found out that he not only left Power Academy without permission but that he was found skulking around an N.P.C. security guard's home.

I pushed that thought from my mind. "He'll be here." *He has to be*, I thought to myself, forgetting that Ellie obviously knew what I said.

In the background, I heard the clicking footsteps of someone coming down the hall. *Click clack, click clack, click clack.* Clothes-too-tight Larriby always wore soft-soled grandma-esque shoes, so it must be Mayor Masters.

Over here, I thought to Ellie, gesturing her to come my way. There was a slight curve in the hallway where Power Academy met up with N.P.C., and we flattened ourselves against the wall. Just as quickly as we heard the footsteps coming in our direction, the sound of them went farther and farther away.

"Phew," Ellie sighed. "If we get caught—"

"That reminds me of something," I cut her off. "We need to do some super sleuth work. Give me a hand," I said, nodding my head in the direction of the security camera above the door.

Larriby watches those, like, all the time, I said in my head to Ellie.

Okay?

I grabbed the bottle of black nail polish from my pocket and shoved it in her face.

"Oh, I get it."

"You're much taller," I said, while she grabbed the bottle from my freshly painted nails. In two jumps, she had painted over the camera's lens.

I impatiently tapped my foot on the ground below. *Where is—*

"Ah!" I jumped, feeling a tap on my shoulder.

"You scared the you-know-what out of me," I said to Logan, who now miraculously stood in front of me. An access card suspended from a long lanyard dangled from his right hand. My dad's bald-headed face stared back at me.

"You got it!" I said and lurched forward, embracing Logan in a hug.

"Oh. Em. Gee. This is totally awesome!" Ellie squealed, joining in on the hug. I pulled away. "I love all this secret spy stuff," she said.

Logan and I rolled our eyes simultaneously. Oh, Ellie. She added an element of levity to this serious situation. We would be grounded for life for breaking into Nova Power Corporation.

"I think you should do the honors," Logan said, placing the card in my hand, which now shook with nerves.

"But what if it doesn't work?" I asked.

"There's only one way to find out."

I lifted the card to the thin slot on the box and pulled down. The red blinking light turned green. We were in.

Chapter Nineteen

It was like we walked into a completely different world as the glass door swished closed behind us. Nova Power Corporation contrasted with Power Academy—and the rest of Nova, for that matter—in every way.

Where there was a grand entrance to Power Academy, complete with a sparkly, shiny chandelier and new green wallpaper, N.P.C.'s walls were gray. There were no lights whatsoever, except for the dim emergency lights that lined the baseboards on the floor.

"I wish Sam were here to give us some light," Ellie muffled. I could hear the sadness in her voice.

"That's why we're here," Logan reassured her. I smiled

at his kind words. Cute, funny, and nice. What else could a girl want in a boyfriend? I mean … friend. What else could a girl want in a friend that just so happens to be a boy?

"I threw this in for good measure," Logan said, reaching into his back pocket and pulling out a small flashlight. *And smart*, I thought to myself. Ellie nudged me in the shoulder, reading the thoughts right from my head.

As we continued down the hallway, we passed by offices and more offices. The first door read *Office of Nova Transportation*. Then we got to the *Office of the Treasurer*. A small door to the right read *Security*. Even though I never saw where my dad worked, I knew that his home base was behind that door. He had done security for the city of Nova for over twenty years. I sighed.

"Poppy, it's okay," Logan said, taking my hand in his. "You had to do it."

Was the guilt over taking my dad's security access card showing that much?

"Yes, it is showing that much," Ellie answered. Typical Ellie move.

"This is all to help our friends," Logan said, squeezing my hand gently and then letting go. I wished he hadn't let go.

"This is totally ridiculous," Ellie huffed. "Just one hall

after another." She threw her hands up. "I don't even know what we're looking for!"

We turned a corner just to be greeted by another equally long hallway. I wasn't sure exactly what we were looking for, either, but I had an odd feeling that I would know once we saw it.

"Well, we only have tonight," I said, dangling the access card in front of her face. "Logan has to get this back before the morning so my dad doesn't notice it's gone."

At the end of that second hallway, we took a right turn, and, again, saw another long hall. But something was different about this one. The other hallways were pitch black, but there was a soft, flickering glow, similar to the glow of a television, at the end of this one.

"Shhh, I think someone's coming," Ellie said, stopping in her tracks.

We all grew still. "I don't hear anything," Logan said.

"Neither do I."

"Sorry, guys," Ellie said. "False alarm."

The light grew more and more pronounced as we continued down the hall, and I could finally see where it was coming from—behind a large glass door at the end of the corridor. We were almost at the door when I turned around. Logan was right behind me, but Ellie was still standing at the far end.

"I don't know about this," she whispered loudly. "Something just seems … off." Even with the distance between us, I could tell she was shaking from nerves.

Ellie, please. We'll probably find nothing, but at least we tried, I thought down to her. *Let's just check it out, and then we'll go back.* She sighed and walked towards us.

All together now, we stood at the end of the hall in front of the giant metal door with the words *Testing Center* written on the front. Although I had no idea what was behind those doors, I knew that it was something that we needed to see.

With a quick swipe of the card, we were in.

I looked around the sterile room. Against the far wall was a ginormous shelving unit enclosed behind glass that looked about two-inches thick. Rows upon rows of medical equipment were stacked on the shelves—test tubes, IVs, needles, gauze, and what looked to be surgical equipment.

The floor matched the feeling I got as we entered—cold and gray. I couldn't believe it when I saw him. Off to the far side of the room sat Mark Masters. Gone was the nose-picking-extraordinaire son of Mayor Masters that I knew. He was pale and a few beads of sweat trickled down his head. Nerves had obviously overtaken him. He rocked back and forth, back and forth, gripping his left arm with the opposite hand.

He looked awful.

As I walked closer to him, he looked up at me, but it was almost as if he looked through me, like he wasn't registering that I was even there.

"They don't know that I'm here," Mark said, continuously glancing back at the door behind him.

"Who doesn't know, Mark?" I asked.

Silence.

I stepped closer to him. "Mark, who doesn't know?"

"*I* just don't care about not being a weekday. I just don't care that much." He turned his head and looked me directly in the eyes when he spoke the next words. "Get them away from me."

"Mark, you're not making sense," Logan said, taking both of Mark's shoulders in his hands and gently shaking him.

"Get him some water," I shouted back to Ellie.

She used her cusp power to telekinetically fill a beaker of water and lobbed it into my hand.

"Here," I said, pushing the liquid into Mark's face. "Drink this."

He mechanically reached up, grabbed the cup of water,

and sipped. But Mark's odd behavior continued. "*She* just doesn't care!" he shouted. A sip of water obviously didn't do the trick. He quickly fell right back into his trance.

"Who, Mark? Who doesn't care?" Logan prompted.

"Move," Ellie demanded, taking a step forward, another beaker of water tight in her grasp. In an instant, she lurched her hands forward and the water flew out of the glass and into Mark's face. His head jerked from side to side a few times and then stopped.

"Mark?" we all asked in unison.

"What did you do that for?" he asked, coming back to reality.

"Mark?" Ellie said, placing her manicured hand on his shoulder.

"Oh … hey, Ellie," he said, as if seeing her for the first time tonight. He took a few long blinks, glanced around the room, and then it was like it all clicked. He stood up in an instant.

"You guys need to get out of here. Now!" he spoke, pushing Logan toward the door.

"We aren't going anywhere," Logan said, pushing him right back down into his chair. "You need to tell us what's going on!" Logan sounded downright mad.

"Where are Sam and Sabrina?" Ellie asked, taking the

thought right out of my head.

"They're here, too. Well, not here, here. But here at N.P.C. Somewhere." Mark's eyes darted to the clock above the door—8:57 p.m.

"They'll be back soon. You can't be in here when they come."

"Who?"

"They always come back at nine."

"Who, Mark?"

"Just get out of here. Hide in that closet," he said, pointing at a white door with a silver handle on the other side of the room.

"Wait," Ellie said. "Before we go anywhere, I want to know what's going on in this ..." she shivered, "place."

Mark's eyes darted to the clock again. 8:59 p.m. "Go!" he shouted.

That was enough to make us all hurry into the tiny closet—and just in time. As we ducked inside, the *beep, beep, beep* access sounded. The door to the room unlatched and then clicked back in place. Although everything was a bit muffled, I could make out three voices. Mark's, a man's I didn't recognize, and Mark's mother. Mayor Masters.

Chapter Twenty

We couldn't make out what was being said on the other side of the closet door, and there were too many thoughts going back and forth to decipher what was being said. But there was shouting—I was sure of that. And I think it was Mark who was doing the shouting. After what seemed to be at least fifteen minutes, we heard the door open and then click shut. Ellie, Logan, and I stumbled out of the tiny room.

"What was that all about?" I asked.

Mark rocked back and forth, back and forth in the chair once again. He was in the same state of mind we found him in when we first entered this creepy room.

Ellie grabbed my shoulder. "What if we head back to Power Academy? I just feel like we need to tell someone about …" her voice trailed off as she looked around the room. "This. Whatever this is."

We were onto something here, and there was no way we were going back to Power Academy without at least trying to get some answers.

"Water," I said to Ellie.

Splash! Water dripped to the floor below.

Just like that, Mark snapped out of it.

"Sorry, guys," he said, shaking off his stupor.

"Well?" I asked. "What did they want?"

Mark fidgeted with the ends of his sleeves. "I shouldn't be telling you," he said through gritted teeth. He glanced up at the clock.

"Telling us what?" Logan asked, pushing a piece of hair from his face.

Mark didn't respond.

"Telling us what?" Logan asked, louder this time.

"They hooked me up to this … this …"

I attempted to read his mind but to no avail. His thoughts just weren't coming to me.

"They hooked you up to?" Logan asked.

I shot him a don't-rush-him kind of look.

Getting information out of Mark was proving to be difficult. Mark looked to the rows of test tubes behind the thick glass.

"This machine," he whispered. "They roll it in and then roll it out, put these needles in my arms, and then …" He paused and swallowed so loud I could hear the spit go down. Two fresh Band-Aids rested in the crease of his elbow. He continued. "Then they ask me to do stuff with weekday powers."

Ellie's nose scrunched. "What do you mean, do stuff with weekday powers?" Ellie asked. "You're a Saturday."

"And that's exactly the point!" Mark shouted. "My mother *hates* that I'm a powerless nobody. I'm not a weekday. I'm not a stupid Monday, Tuesday, Wednesday, Thursday, or Friday. I'm just—"

"Mark, we're here to help you," I said, placing a hand on his shoulder in an attempt to calm him down. He was rambling. Whatever they were doing to him was so bad that he could barely hold on to a thought. Mark's words were all over the place.

"Please start at the beginning," I said, forcing a smile for Mark's sake.

"Why do you all even care at all?" he asked. "It's not like you ever gave me the time of day at Nova Elementary or Nova Middle." He nodded his head toward Ellie. Gosh, that was harsh. But true. I thought back to elementary school and when he had been labeled "the nose-picker of Nova".

"Digging for gold, are we?" Ellie had asked him a number of times, jabbing an elbow into his side. She had changed over the last year, though. Gone are her mean days.

"I am truly sorry, Mark." *I am*, she thought in her head. And I believed her.

"Really, I am," she said out loud, this time.

And it was enough for Mark to go on, even though I read his thoughts, and he was anything but accepting of her apology.

He shook his head—like he was shaking away the years of torment. "Thank you," he said, looking down at his hands. There was an awkward silence and then Mark took one big breath. And he began.

"My mom's crazy," he began. "She's been obsessed about me being a weekend forever." He paused. "Well, obsessed with me *not* being a weekday is more like it."

We all knew that. In fourth grade, Mayor Masters had made a big deal about Mark being made fun of while all the other weekdays were coming into their powers. She was tired of him being bullied, so she was the one who decided that there would be no power usage in the school system—not for *all* to appear equal, but for her son to appear equal. Although ridiculous, who would question that decree from the mayor?

Mark stilled and continued, the real Mark returning. "Anyway, mom never understood why only weekends were powerless. She wanted me to have powers just like everyone else." He chuckled, thinking back to something. "And my aunt even told me that mom tried so bad to keep me from being a weekend. She apparently tried to bribe the nurses to deliver me early so I could at least be born a disappearing Friday." He frowned. "That was before she was mayor. If she was mayor then, I probably would have been a Friday."

So it was true. Moms really did go out of their way to give birth on certain days.

I felt so bad for Mark Masters, the nose-picking extraordinaire of Nova. We'd all seen Mayor Masters's looks of disappointment at times, but she was always so nice to me. To us.

As I looked at the beaten-up Mark sitting in front of me, it was obvious she was anything but nice. I could only imagine how hard she was on poor Mark. Did his mom even love him?

"So what does this have to do with this …" Logan

glanced around the room, "place?"

Mark looked toward the cement floor. "They're experimenting," he said, barely audible.

The whites of Ellie's eyes grew larger. "What do you mean, experimenting?" It sounded like something right out of a science fiction movie.

"Wait ... but Headmistress Larriby said you're doing some sort of internship here?" I asked.

"Obviously, that's a lie," he said, looking me square in the face. "My mom's been telling lies to everyone." He shook his head. "She actually convinced my dad that I was sent to London to a special power school, where my sister Maggie actually went years ago. See," he said, lifting his hands in exasperation. "Even Headmistress Larriby thinks I'm here for some internship. And don't even get me started on that awful Fluxnut guy."

"So, Mr. Fluxnut knows about this too?" I asked.

"Yes, he's the one keeping tabs on all of you," he said, his eyes darting to the clock.

Now Mr. Fluxnut's creepiness was making sense. The whole acting thing was probably just an excuse to keep an eye on us. Not an eye for protection, though.

"Anyway, they come in here, and inject me with this ... this ... stuff," he said, pointing at the vials in the locked glass cabinet behind him.

"And what does it do?" Logan asked.

"Mom thinks it's supposed to give me weekday powers."

I couldn't quite grasp what he was saying. *Supposed* to give him powers. How could that even happen? You had to be born on a certain day, in Nova, to have certain powers. How could that stuff actually give you a power?

"How would that even be possible? You're born with your weekday ability, silly. It isn't something that can just be given to you." Ellie had once again taken the though right from my head.

"Don't you get it?" Mark asked, his eyes growing wider, if that was even possible. "My mom has literally gone crazy. And now she thinks she can take other people's powers and stuff."

"So what has she done with the missing weekdays?" Logan asked.

"Wait. Go back." I hesitated, thinking about what Mark had said. "What do you mean, 'taking people's powers'?"

I shook my head. I had never heard anything like this. If you're born in Nova on a certain day, you are born with certain powers. You have those powers forever. Nobody can "take" them from you. And nobody can just "give" them to you.

"I still don't get it," I said.

Logan grabbed my hand and looked me in the eyes. "I think I do." He looked past Mark and at the glass cabinet. "Nova Power Corporation." His voice was barely audible. "They don't do anything to help us with our powers. They create our powers."

"He's right," Mark chimed in, rubbing his arm.

"No. I was born on a Thursday, so I was born to read people's minds," Ellie said.

"You're wrong," Mark spoke cautiously. He pointed to the cabinet behind him and at the tubes filled with some sort of liquid.

"Oh my gosh," I exclaimed. I walked closer to the locked cabinet and pointed at the letters labeling the tubes. The first cabinet was labeled *M*. The next with *T*. Then *W*, *Th*, and finally, *F*. This couldn't be true.

"I think you get it, Poppy," Mark whispered. He tapped on the glass. "*They* gave you your powers."

Chapter Twenty-One

"And now *she* wants to experiment on those people she took. My mom's crazy, you guys." Mark turned away from the vials of weekday power and sat back down.

Nothing made sense. If this was true, then my whole life was a lie. Really, everyone's life in Nova was a lie. Our teachers taught us since the first grade that in our perfect magical town, you had a power based upon the day of the week you were born. And if that wasn't true, then what else have we been lied to about? I just couldn't wrap my mind around what Mark just revealed to us.

"So when you were born, you were injected with a different serum based upon the day of the week."

"But the meteors—"

Mark's shaking voice cut Ellie off. "Are you even listening to me, Ellie? There was no meteor," he said. I wanted to know, no, *needed* to know more, but we didn't have time to ask him any more questions.

"You guys, they're coming back soon," Mark said, breaking my train of thought. The clock over his shoulder read 9:55 p.m.

"How often do they come for you?"

"Every hour," Mark said. "But it doesn't matter. These serums won't work on twelve-year-olds, but she keeps trying anyway. She's crazy!"

"Mark. You have to tell us where she is taking the cuspers who've disappeared!" I said with urgency. For a moment, the huge bomb Mark dropped on us about his crazy mom and the even crazier origins of our weekday powers distracted me. But even with everything we'd just heard, we had to find Sam and Sabrina—especially if what Mark said about his mom experimenting on them was true.

"What are cuspers?" Mark asked.

"You know—weekdays with two powers." Ellie said, twirling a few strands of hair around her fingers, like that piece of information was the most normal fact in the world.

I could tell by the look on Mark's face that he had

never heard that term before. How could he not know what a cusper was, especially considering that his own mother was a one? That was another confusing part of this whole situation; why was Mayor Masters targeting cuspers, anyway?

Mark gestured toward the door. "All I know is that they're keeping weekdays in the basement to ..." he swallowed. "To experiment on them. But you have to get out of here. Now! Before they come back."

"But how do we even get to the basement?" I asked.

Mark's eyes darted to the lanyard and keycard suspended from my neck.

"Oh!" *Of course.*

"And I'm coming with you," he said, unemotionally.

No one objected. We needed him to lead the way.

"I overheard some of the N.P.C. guys talking about special weekdays and that's how I know where they are," Mark said as we made our way through the windy labyrinth of hallways once again. "Sometimes, I pretend to be really out of it so they say stuff in front of me, not realizing I'm just storing all that information to use at some other time."

"Like now," Ellie said cautiously, probably because of the way he snapped at her a little bit ago.

He stopped and looked at her. "I never thought you'd be the one to help."

I smiled. Mark was smart, which was why he could help us now.

He put both hands up, gesturing for us to stop. "Okay. So around the corner is a door that leads down to the basement. There are guards there now. I might not have any magical powers, but I can distract them so you can get down there. Please be careful. I don't know what they might do to you if you're caught or if they find out I helped you," he said, his voice growing quiet. Who knows what they were doing to poor Mark, or what his own mother would do.

"Now go stand behind there." Mark motioned to a large sculpture of a meteor crashing into the Earth, Nova's town symbol. I cringed at the deception.

Total joke, Ellie thought to me.

"It's show time," Mark said with a wink. And as fast as he bounced out of his little trance earlier, he slipped right back into it.

I peeked out from behind the statue just in time to see him run into a wall. "Where am I?" Mark asked, disoriented. His loud voice bounced from wall to wall. "Where am I?" he yelled, louder this time. Surely one of the guards heard him.

"He's a natural actor," Logan said as we watched him smack face first into another wall. Heck, he almost had me convinced that he was lost. If he were attending Power Academy, he would definitely have a role in Mr. Fluxnut's production.

And then they came. Two security guards with N.P.C. hats rounded the corner, stepped up to Mark, and grabbed him by the elbows.

"This way, young man," the short, round one said as the three of them disappeared down the hallway.

We ran to the giant metal door that those guards were protecting. The top of it read *N.P.C. Personnel Only. Trespassers will be punished.* If trespassing meant that we would find our friends, too bad. We were going.

Ellie tapped my shoulder. "Um, Poppy? Don't you see that sign?"

"We've been trespassing for the past hour. I don't think it really matters at this point." One quick swipe of my dad's card and the door opened, leading to a series of metal steps.

"To the dungeon," I said under my breath.

"I'm not so sure about—"

"We got this far, Ellie. We might as well keep going," Logan said.

When we got to the bottom of the staircase, I saw that my dungeon comment wasn't too far from the truth. The basement was damp with a moldy smell, like the smell of my wet clothes when I accidentally leave them in the washing machine too long.

Total grossfest, Ellie thought to me.

Logan clicked on the flashlight and took the lead as we tiptoed through the cavernous room. I didn't know what we were looking for—perhaps another secret room, door, or sterile chamber like the one Mark was held in.

Poppy, I heard Sabrina say in my head.

And now I was hearing things. Great. But then I realized that Sabrina was trying to communicate with me. She was close by. She had to be.

"They're down here somewhere," I said, taking a few steps forward, ignoring the frightened Ellie. But there were no doors, windows, or anything else to indicate another space, so where was Sabrina speaking from? She's close.

"Look, maybe this was just a bad idea," Ellie said, her fingernails digging into my arms. I could practically hear her teeth chattering in my ear at this point.

"You made it through the haunted forest last year, Ellie. This is just some musty old basement," I reminded her.

"You're right," she said, but didn't lessen her grip.

"Over here!" Logan whisper-yelled from the other side of the cavernous room.

Poppy. I heard Sabrina in my head again, but there was no telling where she—and Sam, for that matter—could be. This was a completely empty basement. And then I heard her again. *Behind the wall.*

Was she serious? Behind the wall? They hid our stuff in some secret shed last year, and now they've taken cuspers— real people, real kids—and hidden them behind walls? I thought back to a story our English teacher made us read last year about a man who was trapped behind a wall in a basement, left to … well … a shiver ran up my spine. What kind of Edgar Allan Poe world did we live in?

"I heard it too," said Ellie, forgetting for a moment that her dominant power was a mind-reading Thursday one.

"Um … does someone wanna let me in on the secret?" Logan said, bumping his shoulder into mine. Sometimes I forgot that he was *not* a mind-reading Thursday.

"We just heard Sabrina say that she's behind a wall, but that doesn't make any sense."

"Yeah, maybe Mark was just making all that stuff up to mess with us," Ellie said hopefully. I wished that everything he told us was a lie, but I knew deep down that Mark was telling us the truth. Mayor Masters was kidnapping cuspers out of what, jealousy? Just because her own son was a powerless weekend. I should have paid more attention to her over the past week.

Logan shook his head. "Maybe there is a false wall somewhere around here."

"Like, how the heck would we know if there is one or not?" Ellie asked, scrunching up her nose.

"Don't ask me," Logan shot right back at her.

"You guys. We have things to do. Cuspers to find," I said, trying to break up their squabble.

"Okay, so each of us needs to take a wall. Knock on it, and if you hear or see something, let the other two know," Logan said, pushing hair from his face. He was so cute when he took charge.

We split up and started knocking away. I wasn't entirely sure of what we were looking for but figured that one of us would know if we were onto something.

Poppy, I heard Sabrina's voice again.

I'm coming, I thought right back to her, knowing that if she were thinking hard enough, she could hear me. But there was something I still didn't get. How could Sabrina, a child from a weekday dad and a weekend mom, have two powers? I hoped maybe it would all be answered in time.

My knuckles started to throb from all the knocking I was doing on these concrete walls, but then I heard something. "Over here, guys!" I said quietly, knowing my voice would echo in this room.

In an instant, Logan was right next to me, and Ellie had to do the non-teleporting Tuesday thing—walk.

"Listen," I said. I brought my hand up to the wall and knocked three times.

"It's hollow," Logan said.

"They're behind this one," I said, gesturing to the wall in front of me. "I'm sure of it," I said confidently.

We looked around the room for any kind of tool that would help us break through the wall—a hammer, a crowbar, *anything*—but it was completely deserted.

"What's that?" Ellie asked, raising a freshly manicured finger toward the ceiling.

Just like in the entrance of N.P.C., there was a blinking black box, but there wasn't an access card slot on this one.

"Great!" Logan said, throwing his arms up in surrender. "Now we'll never be able to get in there."

Poppy! I heard Sabrina say again.

"I hear her too!" Ellie said with excitement.

And that's when Miss Maggie's lesson came back to me. "Yes, we will get in," I said, stepping forward. "Get back."

Logan and Ellie moved out of the way as I lifted my finger toward the wall. *Poppy*, I heard Sabrina in my head. *Hurry up, they'll be back.*

"We don't have much time." I flicked my wrist three times in the direction of the wall, just as I'd seen Miss Maggie do. Nothing.

"What was that about?" Ellie asked, clearly frustrated that whatever I'd tried didn't work.

"I need you to help me," I said. "We need to harness super Monday power."

"What? You're ridiculous," she said, laughing.

"No. I'm serious. We are going to flick our wrists three times and concentrate really hard on breaking through the wall. But I need your help."

"Seriously, Poppy? Do you think that it is actually going to work? Nobody's Monday power can do that." She rolled her eyes.

I thought of Miss Maggie and chuckled to myself at how wrong Ellie was, but I wasn't going to go into that whole story. "Just try, at least."

"Fine," she huffed. "But after it doesn't work, can we

please get out of here and tell someone? I don't wanna get caught!"

"Deal," I said, crossing my fingers that it wouldn't resort to that.

"Okay. So here we go." We lifted our fingers in unison. "And now the flicks. One. Two. Three."

Nothing. I frowned, certain it should have worked.

"Okay, let's go," Ellie said, grabbing my hand and dragging me toward the staircase.

And then we heard it. *Crack.* Just like that, a line formed down the middle of the wall, and then another.

"Again," Ellie said.

I rushed to her side.

We lifted our hands in unison. *One. Two. Three.*

Crack. The line in the wall got larger and then another one appeared. Finally, the cement of the wall crumbled to the ground in a pile of rubble.

"Oh my gosh! We totally just did that!" Ellie shrieked, whipping her head around to me with a huge white grin.

"Shhhh," I said, reminding her of the situation we were in. "Someone might hear us."

We crouched down and climbed through the hole we'd just created. I saw Sam, Sabrina, and one other person I didn't recognize who looked to be a year or two older than us. They were crouched down in the corner of the dirt-covered room. There was a door to their right—I assumed was a bathroom.

Sabrina saw me first. "Poppy," she said. She stood up and ran to give me a hug. "I knew you'd hear me!" she said with a slight smile.

I looked to my right to see Ellie and Sam hugging as well.

"Uh … hey," the boy I didn't recognize said, extending his finger and lighting the entire dirt covered room.

As soon as I saw his face though, I knew him. "Are you the Wed—"

"Wednesday who went missing two years ago?" He finished my sentence and then nodded. "Yes. I'm Mack."

"So, that story Veronica always tells us is totally true," Ellie said, letting go of Sam and turning toward Mack.

"Yeah, and as much as I want to tell you what happened, we need to go now," Mack said, climbing through the hole.

Right before we got to the steps, the door at the top of the stairwell opened and the silhouettes of two men and a woman barreled down the staircase.

Chapter Twenty-Two

Mayor Masters blocked our path. "And just where do you all think you're going?" she grimaced, taking a step closer. The woman standing in front of us looked nothing like the Mayor Masters I knew. Her cheeks were a blotchy red, and she had changed from her usual formal attire into an outfit that made her appear ready for a workout. Black streaks of mascara were smeared down her cheek.

Ellie and Sabrina, we need to do it again, I thought, knowing we all were on the same page. Simultaneously, the three of us lifted our hands and flicked. *One. Two.*

As I was about to think *three*, the two men accompanying Mayor Masters pulled out a black contraption with sparks of electricity running through it.

A Taser, Sam thought to me.

"Come on, now," Mayor Masters snarled. "Since when does a measly twelve-year-old's power trump mine?" She asked, looking at the weapon gripped in the man's hands. She turned her attention back to us. "Did you forget that I run this town?" Mayor Masters snarled. "Just one wrong move, and they'll launch those in your direction." Her eyes narrowed on me. "And I think *you'll* be the first for my little experiment," she said, stepping closer to me. Her skeletal fingers ran through my tangled mess of hair.

"Ouch!" I screamed as her boney hand wrapped around chunks of hair. "Get away from me," I said, pushing her hand from my head. But her grip was tight, so instead of letting go, her fingers wound around my orange strands even tighter.

Using her other hand, she grabbed my wrist and squeezed. "Don't ever think I wouldn't break your little wrist. Snap it like the twig you are." Her eyes seared into mine as her grip became tighter and tighter. "If any of you move," she said, her eyes frantically whizzing from Ellie to Sam to Sabrina, then to Mack, "it only takes one quick twist of my hand or a nod of my head to use the Tasers," she threatened.

Ellie's eyes darted toward the steps, but the two men

blocked any path for escape. Hopefully, Logan would be smart enough to disappear the heck out of here. As if he read my mind, he vanished.

Mayor Masters wasn't even phased by his disappearance. "Now the rest of you, get back in that room," she said. "And Ernest," she turned toward one of the men. "You take care of that Friday boy." Just as fast as Logan disappeared, the man she talked to did as well.

"Now, all of you—go!" she said.

We stumbled through the hole we had just created and back into the small room.

"Yes," Mayor Masters said again, following us through the craggy wall, standing so close to me I could feel her breath on my neck. "I think we will definitely begin with you, Poppy Rose Mayberry."

At this point, my thoughts were in a million different places at once. Would I ever see my family or Pickle again? What would happen to Logan once that awful man working for Mayor Masters caught him? Why had I been told lies my entire life?

An evil, crooked smirk formed on Mayor Masters' face. I had forgotten that she was a mind-reading Thursday, so I was sure she heard the concerned thoughts flying around in my head.

"How did you," she stepped back, "all of you, deserve powers over my poor little Mark?" She laughed maniacally. "All they needed to do was just give him the powers … tell everyone that he was born on a Friday instead of on a powerless weekend day. That's all. It would have been so easy." She looked and spoke to each of us intently, as if we were some jury she needed to convince.

"Nobody …" she continued, "nobody needed to know. And why should prissy little Ellie Preston get a power over my poor Mark? You don't even deserve it. Your mother doesn't even deserve it," she said, now beginning to breathe heavily.

I was scared last summer trying to find Pickle, but that fear was magnified ten times as the crazed Mayor Masters continued. The man standing behind her held his finger on the black device's trigger, ready to launch volts of electricity through the air at us if we tried any kind of escape.

Mayor Masters shook her head from side to side. "It's not fair," she muttered. "It's never been fair." Her head dropped to her chest.

I looked up to see the man holding the stun gun slowly bring it down to his side, pointing it away from us and toward the ground. The breath I didn't realize I'd been holding escaped from my lips.

Suddenly, a silhouette of another figure appeared behind Mayor Masters.

"Mom," Mark said. "Please. Let them go." He placed a hand on his mother's shoulder.

Mayor Masters turned around to face her son. "What do *you* want?" she said between clenched teeth. Now it appeared that her anger was directed toward him.

"Please, mom," he begged. "Just let them go."

"If you were only a weekday, Mark," she said, looking past him and making the *come here* motion with her pointer finger. "Do something about him," Mayor Masters said to the man who had tucked his weapon into a loop on his left hip.

The man stepped forward, and just as he wrapped his hand around Mark's forearm, a commotion sounded from the top of the steps. The door opened and two men ran down them. One tackled the man who had the Taser while the other, someone I couldn't *not* recognize, barreled toward Mayor Masters.

"Dad!" I shouted.

In an instant, light flew from my dad's fingertips. The brightness temporarily blinded Mayor Masters and she instantly stumbled backward.

Another one of Mayor Masters' lackeys ran down the stairs.

"Come on, girls!" Ellie said to me and Sabrina.

We pointed to the guard now standing next to Mayor Masters. *One. Two. Three.* A gush of wind flew from our fingertips and crashed into the large man. He smashed against the cement wall and crumbled to the ground. The Nova City officer with my father rushed over to him and pinned them in place. Not a second later, my father held Mayor Masters' spindly arms behind her back. I could see her scrunching her face, channeling whatever Monday power she had, but it didn't work. My father was too strong for her.

"Get back to Power Academy," my dad shouted to the rest of us. "We'll take it from here."

Sabrina disappeared up the stairs first. Ellie and Sam, holding hands, ran up next. I hesitated and ran over to my dad.

"Get to Larriby's office," Dad shouted. "I'll take care of this, Poppy," he said, his tone angry.

I ran to the top of the stairs and made my way through the maze of hallways through N.P.C. and into, yes, *the safety* of Headmistress Larriby's office.

Chapter Twenty-Three

Logan, Ellie, Sam, and I watched through Larriby's office window as Mayor Masters was escorted out the N.P.C. doors and into the backseat of a police car. I was pretty sure she would be locked up in Nova's Powerless Prison for many years to come. I watched as Mark got into a car with his father. His head dropped to his chest and he seemed to be in that same trance-like state we had seen him in before.

"Poor guy," I said, turning back to my friends.

"I guess he'll no longer be known for picking his nose," Ellie said, bumping shoulders with me. I smiled slightly and rubbed the place on my head where Mayor Masters held me in her death-like grip not too long ago.

"Poppy! Thank goodness!" my dad said, running through the door and wrapping his huge arms around me. I didn't know what to expect from him, but this was not the reaction I anticipated.

"Wait? So I'm not in trouble?" I asked, placing his N.P.C. access card in his hand.

"Not at all, Poppy. Thanks to you and your friends, you've helped close this case for us."

"How did you know where to find us?" I asked.

Dad flipped his N.P.C. access card over and tugged on the shiny clip that attached the card to the lanyard. He held up the tiny piece of metal.

"Is that a tracking device?" Sam asked, pushing his glasses up his nose, squinting.

"Yes, it is, Sam," my dad answered. "But now I believe there are some people waiting for you."

I turned around to see Sam's mom and dad standing outside Larriby's office, tears streaming down their faces. "Sammy!" his dad said, pulling the oversized cowboy hat from his own head and hugging his son.

"I'll be in touch," my dad said to Sam's mother as they left.

Ellie ran after Sam and planted a kiss on his cheek.

Sweet, I read from Sam's mind before he rounded the corner with his parents. I smiled.

"We'll see you later, too," Logan said, nodding at Ellie. And right before they were out of the room, Logan mouthed to me, "I'll text you soon."

I smiled and glanced up to see my dad giving me a knowing glance. "He seems like a nice boy," he said, ruffling my hair. Ugh. Dads.

I took the tiny piece of metal from his hand. "So this is how you found us?"

"Yes, I always have my identification badge on the nightstand, ready to grab before I leave in the morning. I woke up last night for a glass of water and noticed it was missing." He looked at Headmistress Larriby and finished. "So I turned on my computer and tracked it here." His forehead creased. "I knew something serious must be going on."

"And it led you right down to the basement of Nova Power Corporation," Larriby said, finishing his thought.

"Mmhmm. In fact, we'd been hard at work looking for those missing cuspers since well before Sam disappeared," he said, rubbing his head. "And when we got word of Sabrina, we knew that these disappearances were getting closer together." Dad scratched his head. "Never did we think they were being held captive in our headquarters all along." He sighed. "We should have known, though, especially considering the last two disappearances happened next door."

"How many missing cuspers were there?" I asked.

My dad looked at his shoes and then back at me. "There were two other than Mack and your friends."

Before I could even ask the next question, my dad answered it.

"They were found at Mayor Masters' home and are safe now. As soon as the first two went missing, we knew that there was some sort of connection with the cuspers, and naturally, being Mayor, Mayor Masters was alerted of this. So, when she suggested you and your friends come to Power Academy as *counselors*, we assumed it was safe, especially with the new N.P.C. headquarters next door ..." his voice trailed off.

"But what about all the other security people? Wouldn't they have known she was holding Mark there? Experimenting on him?" I asked. There just had to be more to this story.

"It's been revealed that Mayor Masters had been blackmailing key security guards' families into doing some work for her," Headmistress Larriby interjected.

My dad shook his head. "As much as I hate to admit it, Mayor Masters was clever. Keep your enemies close, I guess."

And to think that Mayor Masters saw me and the other cuspers as the enemies. That's why she had N.P.C. join up with Power Academy. So we would be nice and close for her little "experiment."

Poor Mark. She sure had us all fooled.

"Thanks to you and your teleporting friend *borrowing* my card," he cleared his throat, "we cleared up this whole mess." He smiled at me and wrapped his arms around my shoulder once more. "But, Poppy," his tone became serious as he pushed away from me. "What were you thinking? Breaking into Nova Power Corporation? Who knows *what* would have happened if I didn't get there in time."

I shrugged. "Nobody was doing anything about my friends, and it just didn't seem right."

"Very well," he said, accepting my excuse. "I'm just happy you're safe." He hugged me tight.

As it turns out, Mark wasn't lying at all, even though I wasn't sure about the true origin of our powers, yet. Mayor Masters had been so obsessed with her son not being a weekday that she was going to all sorts of extremes to get him some sort of power. She'd been injecting him with those serums we saw in the room where she'd trapped him, which totally didn't work. Once she realized the serums weren't working the way she wanted them to, and her precious son would always be a powerless Saturday, she kidnapped some of the cuspers strictly out of jealousy and then decided that perhaps she could somehow drain the powers out of, gulp, them. Us.

"If my own son is powerless, then why do some petulant little kids get to have two powers?" Mayor Masters had asked my father, kicking and screaming while Nova Power Corporation guards dragged her out of N.P.C. and into the back of the squad car. As much as I hated to admit it, I wanted to know the answer to her question. Why did we have two powers? The whole cusp power thing didn't make sense, especially now that I knew Sabrina's parents' powers, or lack thereof.

Just like dad told me, to pull this all off, Mayor Masters had been manipulating some of the officers at Nova Power Corporation and made it their task to keep an eye not only on her own son, but also Sabrina, Sam, and Mack. She apparently had threatened their jobs and their families if they revealed what she was doing to anyone.

I wasn't surprised to learn that Mr. Fluxnut was in on the whole thing, too. He had been assigned to keep an eye on Ellie, Logan, and Sam, and me. So when Veronica and I had seen him creepily skulking around Novalicious at the beginning of the summer, he was watching me, not trying to protect me.

"I should have done more. I'm truly sorry," Larriby said, shaking her head. I read into her mind and her thoughts solidified her story; I believed her. She didn't know what Mayor Masters was up to.

"It was her goal to experiment on some of them?" Headmistress Larriby asked, tears welling in the corner of her eyes. I was shocked to see her become so emotional. "But why?" she whispered. Her face was bright red. I pointed toward a box of tissues on the windowsill and telekinetically sent it over to her pudgy hand.

"Thank you, Poppy," she said, wiping away the tears from her face. This was a side of Larriby I never thought I'd see. The side that calls me by my first name. The side that has real emotions. I kind of felt bad for her. She actually looked human sitting across from me with ugly-cry face.

"I should have known. The way Mayor Masters insisted that Mr. Fluxnut join Power Academy this summer was just plain odd." She bent her head so that her double chin fell to her chest. "She told me that Mr. Fluxnut was tired of his job at N.P.C. and wanted to pursue a career in the creative arts. And here, he could also assist in the cusper disappearances. And the lies she had me believing! Her son doing an internship." She glanced toward the window and blew her nose. "I was so stupid," she thought aloud.

My dad reached his hand across the table and placed his hand on Headmistress Larriby's. "Mayella—you did everything you could," he said, consoling her. My dad really was a nice guy. It appeared that Larriby might actually have a heart, too.

"And I should have been more proactive as well," my dad said, looking toward me again. "We'd been looking into this situation for a while, and really felt that it was in your and your friends' best interests to remain at Power Academy until we had a better handle on what was occurring. Had I known this was happening right next door—" He couldn't finish his thought.

"It's okay, dad. Really, it is. You saved us," I hugged him hard. "And what about Miss Maggie?" I asked, afraid that she would be implicated in this whole mess as well.

"What's going to happen to her?"

Headmistress Larriby wiped a tear from her cheek before she responded. "Miss Maggie is fine. She, too, was threatened by her own mother. When she found out what her mother was up to, she was forced to keep her mouth shut or get sent back to London indefinitely."

"Oh," I gasped.

"What, Poppy?"

"Dad, it was Miss Maggie who gave me the tool I needed to find those cuspers," I said, thankful for that lesson she so expertly planted in the Monday power intensive class.

"I know," he said with a smile. "She will be rewarded for that."

I debated whether or not to ask him the next question, but did anyway. "And what about our powers and what we found out?" I asked.

"What do you mean, Poppy?"

"You know, how we're not bor—"

"Let's just get you home to see your mom and brother," he said, quickly glancing at Headmistress Larriby. He wrapped his arms around me again, so tight this time that I wouldn't be able to finish the question even if I wanted to. "I know your mom can't wait to see you," he said, changing the subject.

He knew about our powers. He definitely knew what I was talking about.

As we walked out the doors to Power Academy, Pickle in hand, I asked my dad again, "And what about our powers and what we found out?"

He sighed. "Poppy, that is classified information. You really can't let that get out."

"But what does it eve—"

"Poppy," my dad said again, gently squeezing my hand. "You need to let that go."

But I knew, just as I was sure my father knew, that letting go would be a hard thing to do.

Chapter Twenty-Four

One Week Later

Veronica and I were sitting at Novalicious, reading the latest issue of *The Nova Weekday Public Opinion,* Nova's daily newspaper. There were two main headlines on the cover:

Kidnapping? Bribery? Mayor Masters Arrested

and,

Dual Powers? Cuspers Revealed in Nova

It was quite the scandal. Mayor Masters had been arrested for kidnapping, Mr. Fluxnut was being held as an accomplice, and the Nova City authorities were also questioning a few guards. But before she was arrested, Mayor Masters leaked the cusper information to the press. I was actually kind of glad that secret was out.

"So, why couldn't you just tell me you had two powers?" Veronica asked, taking a lick of her cone and then sliding the newspaper across the table. "I wouldn't have been mad."

I used my Monday power to throw the napkin in the trash. "Well, when the mayor tells you not to do something, you kind of have to listen." I looked her in the eyes. "But I felt terrible about it the whole time, Veronica. I wanted to tell you so badly. But I'm still not even sure what it all means." I confessed this to her, only to be lying right to her face yet again. Could I ever tell her that nobody in Nova was born a true weekday? That Veronica's own Monday power was given to her when she was born? That our entire town of Nova, our entire existence, was a farce—some crazy, wacky, giant science experiment that not even my dad would explain to me?

There was so much more I wanted to know, but I didn't know who could tell me. Why Nova? How did they even get the powers? And what was in those serums? And why exactly did I have two powers?

"Hey, girls!" I heard Ellie's voice and turned around

to see her waltzing through Novalicious. Her bright pink jacket swished with each step she took. "Can you believe that about Mayor Masters and poor Mark?" she asked, plopping her giant pink purse in the middle of the table.

"It's crazy," Veronica said, actually looking at Ellie when she spoke. Veronica and I had had a heart-to-heart right after I got back from Power Academy, and she promised to try harder with Ellie. I promised to do the same, but with her. I realized that I maybe wasn't giving Veronica the attention I should give my BFF—I had gotten a little too excited to have a new friend in Ellie.

"I'm still bummed about *A Midsummer Night's Dream*, though," Ellie said, pulling the playbill that was going to be handed out at the final performance from her bag.

"But what about the play?" Ellie had asked Larriby right before we were sent home, as if that was the most important thing to think about at the time. Not that we'd just uncovered the biggest secret in the town of Nova, or anything.

"That was a distraction Mayor Masters set for you all. But obviously it wasn't distracting enough," Larriby had said with a smile. "Ellie, there will be plenty of other acting opportunities for you at Nova Middle." I knew that was the truth.

"Anyway," Ellie said, looking toward the ice cream

counter. She flicked her wrist, and the chocolate syrup floated through the air and landed on our table. "At least I can do *that* now," she said with a smirk. "Without getting weird looks."

Both Veronica and I rolled our eyes. *Typical Ellie*, Veronica thought to me.

"Hey, I heard that," Ellie said, through a smile. "Remember, I still read minds."

"Great, two mind-reading friends."

Friends.

Buzz. I pulled my purple rhinestone cellphone from my pocket to see that I had one message from Logan.

`Logan: Meet me in ten at Nova El.`

I couldn't hide the smirk. "Girls, I gotta go."

"*Looooh-gan*," they said in unison, making kissy faces at me.

"Um ... no," I said, rolling my eyes at them.

When I got to the playground at Nova Elementary, Logan was nowhere to be found. It would be just like him to scare the heck out of me by popping up in the middle of nowh—

"Ahhhh!" I screamed, as Logan appeared next to me. "Do you always have to do that?"

Logan smiled that adorable crooked smile that I like so much. A piece of hair covered his eye, so I lifted my hand and brushed it out of the way. Why use my power when I could just use my hand?

"I have to show you something," he said, grabbing my wrist and pulling me to the metal bus jungle gym that I used to play on in third grade.

"Um, okay …" I said, confused. "It's a bus."

"I just don't want anyone to see," he whispered. "Come on."

He ducked inside the yellow structure and I followed behind.

"Okay, hold my hands tight, like really tight."

I did as he said. I hoped he didn't notice the nervous clamminess sticking to my fingers.

He took a deep breath. "Now close your eyes."

I shut them tight.

I wasn't one hundred percent sure what would happen next, but I thought that I had a pretty good idea. I mean, we both definitely liked each other; I just didn't think my first kiss would be in an old, metal, rusted-up bus.

Then he started counting. With each number he squeezed my hands tighter and tighter.

"One. Two." His face was super close to mine on that final count. "Three."

And nothing happened. No kiss on the cheek. No kiss on my face at all.

"Okay," he whispered in my ear. "Now open your eyes."

My jaw practically dropped to the ground. "Oh my gosh."

I looked around the familiar setting. We no longer sat in a pretend school bus. The entrance steps to Power Academy felt hard under my butt—steps that were on the other side of town.

"Did we just … " I couldn't finish the thought. But I knew it was real.

I had just teleported with Logan. I didn't know why or how. But this was pretty much the most fantabulous thing ever.

Acknowledgements

A HUGE thank you to the fans and readers of *Poppy Mayberry*. Your emails, letters, pictures, and overall excitement over *Poppy* is exactly why I wrote her story. Thank you for reading and loving Poppy, Pickle, and friends!

Thank you to my parents who always support and encourage me to do what I love. Thanks to my family, friends, colleagues, and students for so enthusiastically supporting me and my writing.

I am forever grateful to my editor Tara Creel and her amazing support and guidance while writing *Poppy*. Tara – you are a rock star editor. Thanks to my *Poppy* series agent, Bill Contardi and all the agents at Brandt & Hochman. And a huge thank you to Georgia McBride for making my publishing dreams come true.

A huge shout out for the amazing group of YA and MG authors in the Sweet Sixteens debut group who continue to encourage one another. To my Sixteen to Read sisters – your support through this wonderful, yet roller coaster of a publishing experience is so important to me. I love you girls!

Finally, again, a special thank you to my husband. Even though you make fun of my "teeny-bopper" TV viewing habits and my ramblings about crazy middle-grade ideas, I could not successfully juggle a full-time teaching job and a writing career without the support of you and our amazing son, Bennett. So to both of you – thank you for holding down the fort while I have my "write time" during many evenings and weekends. I love you both to the moon!

Jennie K. Brown

Jennie K. Brown is an award-winning high school English teacher, freelance magazine writer, and author of children's books. She currently serves as past-president of the Pennsylvania Council of Teachers of English and Language Arts (PCTELA) and is an active member of SCBWI, NCTE, and ALAN. When she's not teaching or writing, Jennie can be found reading, hanging out with her awesome family, or plotting her next book. Learn more about Jennie at jenniekbrown.com!

OTHER MONTH9BOOKS TITLES YOU MIGHT LIKE

POPPY MAYBERRY, THE MONDAY

POLARIS

Find more books like this at http://www.Month9Books.com

Connect with Month9Books online:

Facebook: www.Facebook.com/Month9Books

Twitter: https://twitter.com/Month9Books

You Tube: www.youtube.com/user/Month9Books

Blog: www.month9booksblog.com

Monday isn't just another day of the week.

Poppy Mayberry,
The Monday

NOVA KIDS BOOK 1

Jennie K. Brown

Don't open the door.
Don't invite him in.
He is not from here.

Polaris

BETH BOWLAND

Made in the USA
Middletown, DE
27 December 2018